Rock Climbs in the Sou[th]

WYE VALLEY

Volume 1 Wintour's Leap/Symonds Yat Western Cliffs
John Willson/David E. Hope

Published by Cordee, Leicester

In memory of
Martin Beeken and Grant Kinghorn

© John Willson, David E Hope and Cordee
SBN 0 904405 06 0
First Edition 1977 by Cordee, Leicester

Designed by Mike Dunmore
Printed by Joseph Ward & Co (Printers) Ltd, Dewsbury

If you would like to receive our book lists regularly please write to

Cordee, 249 Knighton Church Road, Leicester, England

Contents Wintour's Leap

5	General Preface
10	Acknowledgements
11	Author's Note
16	Introduction
21	Technical
22	Recommended Climbs
23	Historical
27	The North Wall Area
34	The Great Wall
37	The Central Bay
44	The South Bay
49	Deceiver Buttress
50	The Far South Bay
55	Go Wall
64	Fly Wall
73	First Ascents
77	Index
80	Appendix
83	The Lancaut Nature Reserve
83	Camping and Accommodation
84	Rescue Arrangements

Diagrams and Photographs

8	Wye Valley Area Map
12	North Wall to South Bay (diagram)
14	Far South Bay to Go Wall (diagram)
15	Fly Wall (diagram)
24	North Wall and Great Wall (photo)
40	Central Bay to Go Wall (photo)
66	Fly Wall (photo)

Contents Symonds Yat, Western Cliffs

- 5 General Preface
- 86 Acknowledgements
- 87 Author's Note
- 87 Introduction
- 90 Situation and Approaches
- 91 Technical
- 91 Recommended Climbs
- 92 Historical
- 94 The Introductory Rocks
- 97 The Isolate Buttress
- 98 The Hollow Rock Area
- 105 White Wall and Waterpipes Area
- 110 The Longstone Area
- 113 The Bowlers Hole
- 117 The Far South Buttress
- 120 Index

Diagrams

- 8 Wye Valley Area map
- 88 Hollow Rock, White Wall and Waterpipes Areas
- 89 The Longstone and Bowlers Hole Area
- 123 New Routes

General Preface

Few major climbing areas can have remained so underrated for so long as the Wye Valley. Since the last edition of the Gloucestershire Mountaineering Club's 'Rock Climbs in the Wye Valley and the Cotswolds' (which contained little more than one tenth of the routes in the present volume) just over ten years ago, various attempts at producing a comprehensive guide have failed to get off the ground. An interim guide to Wintour's Leap published by the B.M.C. in 1971, has been unobtainable for some time, and another to Wyndcliffe by Frank Cannings became absorbed into the South East Wales Guide. The Symonds Yat district remained unrepresented. As a result of the vastness and complexity of the area and of the diversity of the different cliffs and their respective histories of development, this new work is not one homogeneous guide so much as two independently prepared ones, each with its own ancillary sections. However, an effort has been made to achieve acceptable compatibility and to avoid unnecessary duplication of the technical sections.

Numerous minor quarries and outcrops will be found scattered around the Valley, and the Forest of Dean and the Cotswolds, several not marked on the OS map, which provide short scrambles and harder problems. Most useful of these, perhaps, are Cockshoots Quarry (also known as Deer's Leap), 162 : 548972, a mile to the north of Wintour's Leap, which tends to stay dry when Wintour's Leap is too wet; and a line of cliffs along the summit of Cleeve Hill, 163 :985266, above Cheltenham, which, though too loose in places to allow safe leading, provide excellent technical and fitness training.

Two substantial omissions will be noticed. Ban y Gor is half a mile north of Wintour's Leap and is well viewed from Wyndcliffe. About a dozen routes were made in 1970 by Frank Cannings and by Clive Horsfield, but as the cliff is part of a Scheduled Site of Scientific Interest and the landowner does not wish to allow access to the land, general agreement has been reached to accept a voluntary ban on climbing until such a time as future conditions allow.

Wyndcliffe itself, though geographically in the Wye Valley, has for some years been covered by the South East Wales Guide. As that book is now being revised and is shortly to be reprinted there seemed little point in covering the crag twice. Here also access problems have recently arisen, and as this volume is likely to appear in print before the S.E.Wales Guide, a paragraph is appended below setting out the situation.

Indeed, as will be seen from almost every section of this book, access has become the climber's major headache in the Wye Valley. Areas designated as an SSSI have a certain amount of protection under Section 23 of the National Parks Act, 1949.

General Preface

The recent Conservation of Wild Creatures and Wild Plants Act (1975) reinforces such protection and is particularly relevant to the Wye Valley. This is rated by the Nature Conservancy as one of the most valuable areas of its type in the country. The rarer flora and fauna are relict survivors of formerly more abundant species, which, because of the lack of human interference, have remained while disappearing elsewhere. Unfortunately these occur only in fairly low numbers and are therefore very vulnerable.

There are some hopes that the situation at Seven Sisters may improve, while Ban y Gor and the Forbidden areas at Wintour's Leap seem unlikely to be open to climbers within the foreseeable future. It has not been our business as guide book writers to conduct access negotiations, though inevitably we have been drawn into the process both officially and unofficially, and we have tried to build up good relations with the other interested bodies. Nor is it our business to decree where climbers shall or shall not climb: we can only state—objectively and with some authority—that the more climbers observe the restrictions described in this volume the more likely it is that closed areas will be opened and unrestricted ones will remain so.

Finally, as in all likelihood this guide will soon be out of date, a second volume is already in preparation in order to cover other crags in the valley and to include any additions to the two crags described in this guide.

D.E.H.
J.W.   January 1977

The Wyndcliffe-Blackcliff Forest Nature Reserve

The crags of Wyndcliffe and Blackcliff lie within this Nature Reserve which is also a Site of Special Scientific Interest and is owned by the Forestry Commission.

Until recently climbing has been restricted to the two areas mentioned in the South East Wales Guide of 1973. These are between Strike and Purple Haze on the Left Hand Crag, and between The Gully and Cardiac on the Right Hand Crag of Wyndcliffe. No climbing was allowed elsewhere on the Reserve. The Nature Conservancy also required climbers to keep to the waymarked footpaths in the Forest, and to ensure that as little vegetation as possible was removed from the cliff while climbing.

Unfortunately, excessive gardening has occurred on the climbing areas and the restricted areas, in spite of clearly worded details in the 1973 guide. Such selfish behaviour was bound to have repercussions and can only be condemned. The Nature Conservancy has expressed concern about the damage and so has the Forestry Commission. This concern is expressed by the possibility of a permit system being introduced by the Forestry Commission. The Nature Conservancy will continue to monitor the site and will notify the B.M.C. on future developments.

The information outlined above, stresses again the need for climbers to observe restrictions in areas of delicate access. The end product of such irresponsible action could be the closure of a crag and the loss of some fine climbing.

Finally, we point out that the B.M.C. is against permit systems, and that while negotiations are proceeding, any prejudicial behaviour would of course be slightly unwelcome. We cannot demand good behaviour but we can ask for a little common sense for the common good.

Wintours Leap

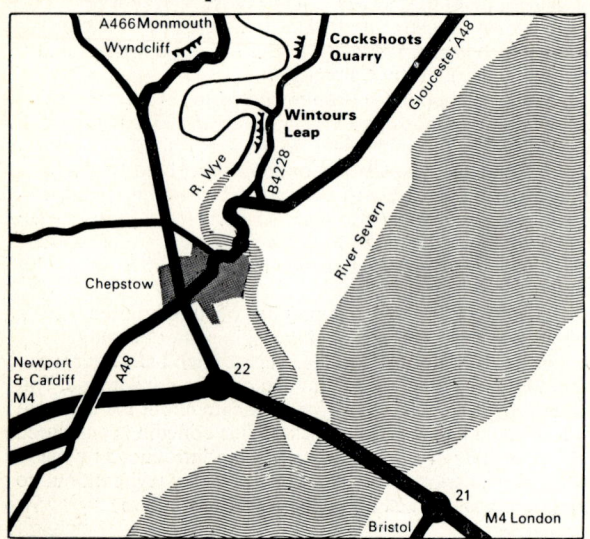

Symonds Yat

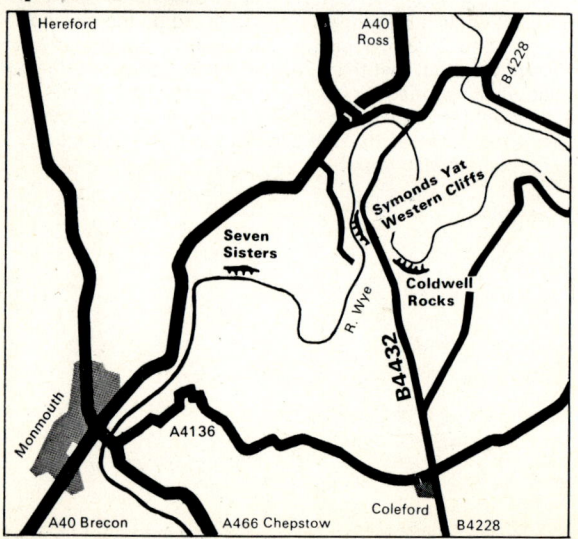

Wintours Leap

Acknowledgements

Although this is a completely new work, its compilation would have been too formidable a task without access to all the information contained in the old Gloucestershire Mountaineering Club pamphlet and Jim Perrin's Interim Guide of 1971. My thanks are due to Chris Rumsey, Tony Pearson, and several members of Rendcomb College Climbing Group for their help in climbing and checking the routes; to Anthony James for unravelling and explaining to me the many mysteries of ownership of the land hereabouts and access to it, as well as for renewing permission for climbers to cross his land on their way off from the North Wall; to Valerie and Ernest Emmett for information about the Lancaut Nature Reserve; to Kathleen James for reading and checking my manuscript; to John Grieve, Keith Williams, and Arni Strapcans for providing information and opinions on the climbs and their grades; and finally to Joe Fivelsdal for the encouragement he has given and for the benefit of his unrivalled knowledge of the cliff.

Author's Note

This is the first comprehensive guide to the cliff, and I have found it necessary to check almost every route personally: therefore, the objective elements—pitch lengths and general descriptions—can be assumed reasonably accurate. However, my limited experience and ability in the hardest climbing must be acknowledged and, as it has not always been easy to obtain much confirmation, the subjective elements—grades and star ratings—may occasionally lack the degree of authority one would wish. I can only say that where other reliable opinions have been available they have shown a substantial measure of uniformity and vindcation of my own assessments. On a large limestone cliff such as Wintour's Leap, much of which has seen little traffic but may well now start to see more, substantial changes may occur: holds, pegs, and vegetation can appear and disappear with disarming rapidity. It is hoped that a revision of the guide will be possible in the not too distant future, and in order that at least that can be definitive it would be helpful if descriptions of new routes, any details or opinions relevant to existing ones, and any information concerning the First Ascent list could be entered in the new log book kept behind the bar in The Rising Sun and/or sent to me at the address below. In contrast with several new 'slimline' guides this work may be found old-fashioned and long-winded. I make no apology for this: the object has been to provide the maximum information about a complex but little known area, which nevertheless has tremendous potential for a wide variety of cimbers. Details found superfluous when the cliff becomes more generally familiar and the features better marked can be omitted from the revision.

J. Willson, Rendcomb College, Cirencester, Glos.

◀ North

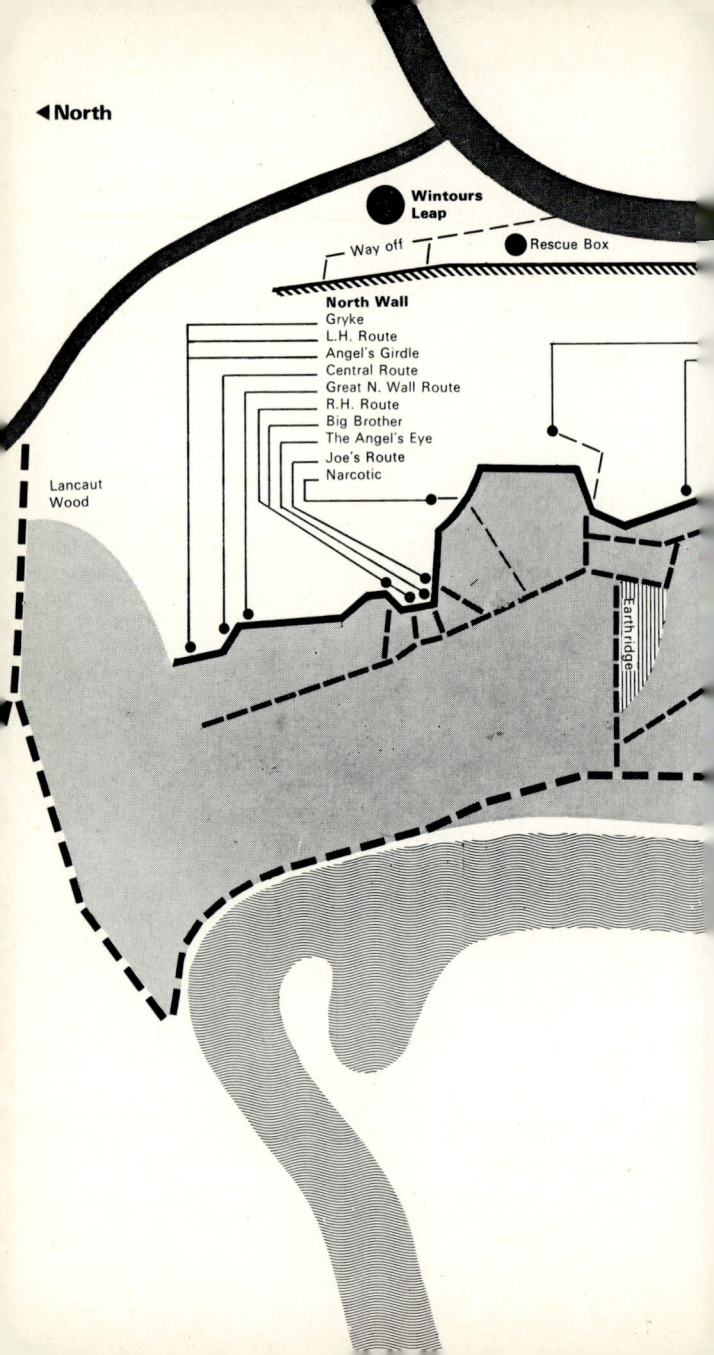

Wintours Leap

Way off — Rescue Box

North Wall
Gryke
L.H. Route
Angel's Girdle
Central Route
Great N. Wall Route
R.H. Route
Big Brother
The Angel's Eye
Joe's Route
Narcotic

Lancaut Wood

Earth ridge

B4228

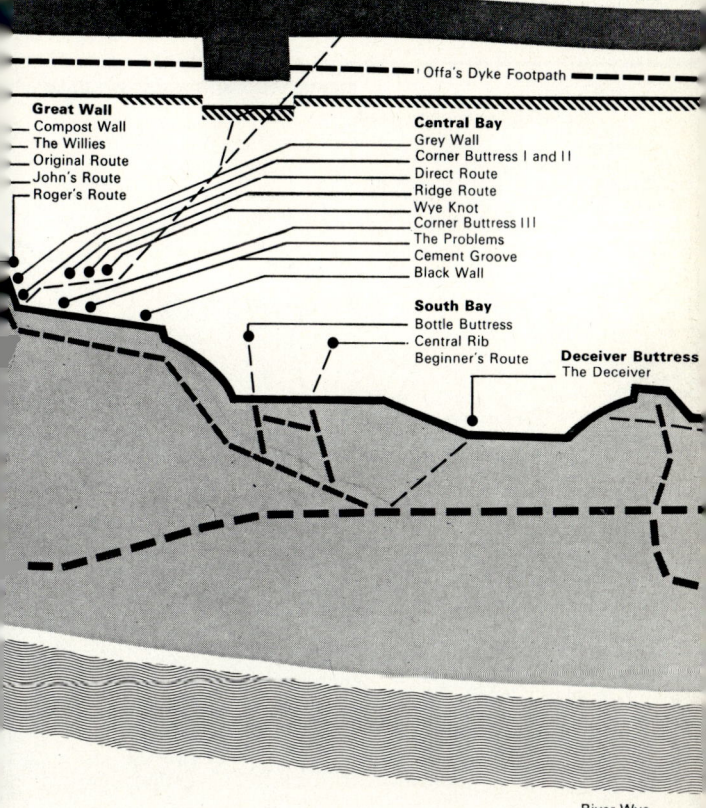

Offa's Dyke Footpath

Great Wall
- Compost Wall
- The Willies
- Original Route
- John's Route
- Roger's Route

Central Bay
- Grey Wall
- Corner Buttress I and II
- Direct Route
- Ridge Route
- Wye Knot
- Corner Buttress III
- The Problems
- Cement Groove
- Black Wall

South Bay
- Bottle Buttress
- Central Rib
- Beginner's Route

Deceiver Buttress
The Deceiver

River Wye

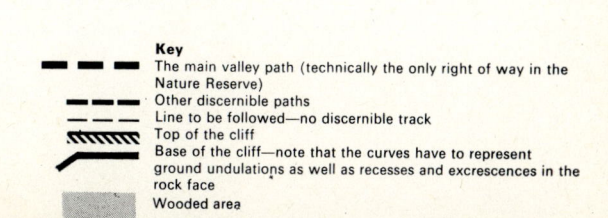

Key
- The main valley path (technically the only right of way in the Nature Reserve)
- Other discernible paths
- Line to be followed—no discernible track
- Top of the cliff
- Base of the cliff—note that the curves have to represent ground undulations as well as recesses and excrescences in the rock face
- Wooded area

Far South Bay
Greta
Zelda
Guytha

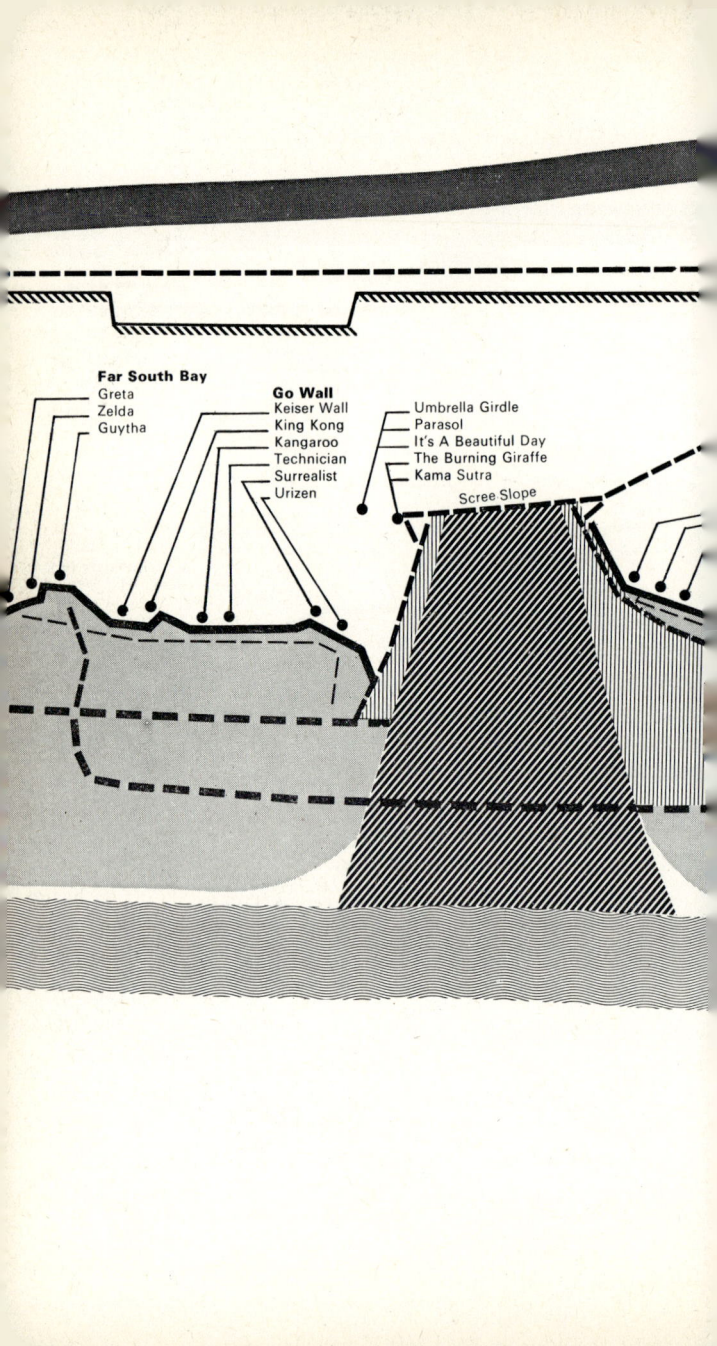

Go Wall
Keiser Wall
King Kong
Kangaroo
Technician
Surrealist
Urizen

Umbrella Girdle
Parasol
It's A Beautiful Day
The Burning Giraffe
Kama Sutra
Scree Slope

Phone Rising Sun Inn

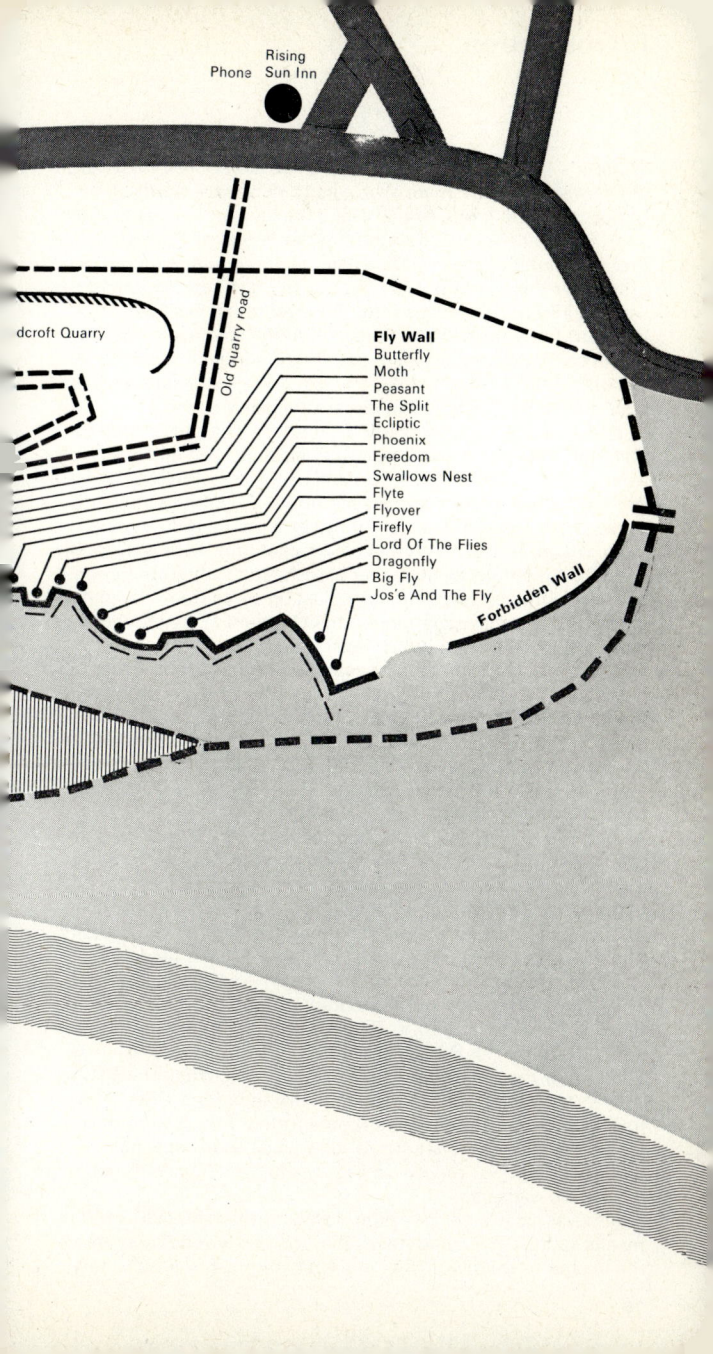

dcroft Quarry

Old quarry road

Fly Wall
Butterfly
Moth
Peasant
The Split
Ecliptic
Phoenix
Freedom
Swallows Nest
Flyte
Flyover
Firefly
Lord Of The Flies
Dragonfly
Big Fly
Jos'e And The Fly

Forbidden Wall

Introduction

Wintour's Leap OS 1 : 50,000 sheet 162 : 542958-64 rises from the east bank of the River Wye one to two miles north of Chepstow, where one of the river's final meanders has cut deep into the carboniferous limestone of the Forest of Dean. Probably most of the face has been quarried at some time or other over the last 200 years but activity has now entirely ceased. The name derives from the legend that Sir John Wintour, hotly pursued by Parliamentarian soldiers in 1642, 'galloped in desperation over the shelving precipice, escaped unhurt on the ground below, and got away by swimming the river' to the Royalist stronghold at Chepstow.

In size and geological formation Wintour's Leap has much in common with the Avon Gorge, but although just as accessible from both London and the Midlands (it is only three miles from the M4) it has never achieved the popularity of its sister cliff. Typically of limestone, much of the best climbing is in the Hard Severe to Hard Very Severe bracket, but there is a good selection of climbs in the lower grades, and though there are as yet few Extremes there are more waiting to be done. On the whole the situations are more attractive than at Avon, and (to risk a subjective value judgement) the routes give a wider variety of technical interest. Vegetation abounds but, except in a wet spell, does not necessarily affect the pleasure or safety of the climbing. Loose rock is more often a hazard and the risks must be carefully assessed. Especially on the little climbed routes one must beware of small holds flaking off without warning, while in a few places there is a danger of accidental trundling if discretion is not exercised.

The Lower Wye Valley is well protected by the Welsh hills and the Forest of Dean, and the weather is often unexpectedly good. Especially in a showery situation, when places as near as Lydney and Newport may be heavily affected, Wintour's Leap frequently remains quite dry. The rock tends to be too slippery when wet but dries out quickly, climbing usually being possible within an hour or so.

The village of Woodcroft is situated at the top of the cliff on the B4228 Chepstow to St Briavels road (from which the rock is not visible). The B4228 leaves the A48 Chepstow to Gloucester road at Tutshill, which is one mile from The Rising Sun Inn in Woodcroft and a similar distance from Chepstow town centre, itself little more than a further mile from junction 22 on the M4. There are no parking facilities except that mentioned below; otherwise one has to find a discreet patch on or off the roadside.

The easiest and most revealing descent on a first visit is by means of a path leading down through the woods from above the village to the river bank, mid-way between the cliffs and

Lancaut Farm on the bend to the north. Drive on through the village, round the right hand bend at the end of the long straight stretch, and turn sharp left up a side road sign-posted 'Lancaut'. There is an iron gate at the top of the hill and one more house on the left, then ample room to park, picnic, or even pitch a tent (which does not seem prohibited at present). Walk down the road a short way until a path leads down left marked by a yellow arrow. Fork left just past the remains of lime kilns (another yellow arrow) and emerge below the ruins of the old chapel. From here is a fine panorama of the whole cliff, the different areas of which can be easily identified from the photographs. Some sections are actually higher than they seem, their nether regions being masked by trees, and as the base of the rock is some 100 feet above the river bank the exposure factor is that much increased.

First is the North Wall where there are several good and popular routes in the middle and upper grades. To its right is the deeply recessed Great Wall, which belies its initially impressive aspect, though a trio of routes on the right hand half will provide something worthwhile for most climbers. Next is the Central Bay, the nursery area, very safe and useful for instruction. A non-descript vegetated buttress separates it from the open, sunny South Bay where there are some fine easier routes with harder alternatives. This is bounded on the right by Deceiver Buttress for loose rock enthusiasts, which in turn recedes into the smaller but deeper Far South Bay containing some of the most enjoyable rock and climbing, much neglected, at Wintour's Leap. Now comes the Great Overhanging Wall (Go Wall) towering almost 300 feet: arguably the most impressive piece of rock in the Wye Valley, it boasts the longest, hardest, and most serious routes in the area, of which only the popular King Kong has been accorded the attention deserved; however, Kangaroo Wall is a must for all competent 'extreme' leaders. Across the scree slope is Fly Wall with some short entertaining V.S. routes on the left half and some longer, harder climbs further right. This is the limit of the climbing area. The Forbidden Wall immediately right of Fly Wall and, further south and lower down, the Pool Cliff and Amphitheatre Buttress all lie within private land with no public right of access to either top or bottom of the cliff. Not only is climbing absolutely forbidden by the owners, but there are strong ecological reasons why these areas should remain undisturbed by Homo Sapiens. This is a pity as several routes are of interest and quality (mostly H.V.S.), but climbers must keep a sense of perspective. First ascent prospectors, please note (see appendix) that most of the lines have been done, while others should find enough to keep them going for a while elsewhere on the cliff.

Introduction

The Wye Valley path, after descending from the road as described, runs the length of the cliff between its base and the river bank, and all the climbs can be reached from it. For the **North Wall,** follow the river bank until the path finally rises from it when almost level with the Great Wall. At the top of this short slope turn left into the woods and go up and along a level earth ridge—a sort of 'long barrow'. From its far end turn left into a clearing and follow the obvious track round. For the raised left half of the **Great Wall** (Compost Wall), almost immediately after turning left off the earth ridge mentioned above, turn sharp right up a steep path which leads leftwards over grass and rock tiers to the foot of the wall proper. For the right half, descend the right side of the earth ridge and take the path which leads first towards the rock and then up round to the right below it, finally reaching the foot of the normal Easy Way Down on the **Central Bay.** The same point can be attained more directly by a track which climbs a steep bank a few yards to the right of the river end of the earth ridge. The track now runs below the Central Bay, descends again into the trees, and emerges in a clearing below the **South Bay** where it rejoins the parent Wye Valley path.

Meanwhile, the latter, from the point where it was left for the earth ridge, has crossed some fallen trees and taken another short rise to the junction just mentioned. **Deceiver Buttress** is reached by scrambling over boulders to the right from here. Further along the path a gap in the vegetation on the bank on the left marks the brambly way to the **Far South Bay.** Further still, well past the remains of a kissing gate, the path forks: straight on is now a cul-de-sac, and the left fork leads up onto the scree slope; the **Go Wall** lower climbs are reached by turning more sharply left into the huge wooded basin, or more directly along a diagonal trough from the kissing gate remains. For the starting ledge of the upper climbs go up the left margin of the scree and turn left. (The top can be reached from here; walk up right through the quarry.)

The left end of **Fly Wall** is just across the top of the slope, while the right end is best reached by crossing down at the bottom. To do this it is necessary to retrace steps to the point where the Far South Bay track left the path: just opposite the gap a good path (yellow arrow again) drops steeply down the bank, crosses the scree, and rises again to a longer level section. Continue along until the buddleia on the left gives way to trees and go straight up to the rock between the two. (A rather useless tunnel through the buddleia connects the top of the scree with the path at the top of the rise—belly work in the growing season.) The path now rises gently below the Forbidden Wall and curves round to the left behind it, passes

under a wooden foot-bridge, and emerges onto the road, south
of the village, through a kissing gate.

It is possible, of course, to do the whole tour in reverse and
this would be the obvious procedure for anyone walking up
from Tutshill. The kissing gate is identified as the lower of two
small iron gates marked 'Offa's Dyke' at the foot of the short
hill below The Rising Sun, just inside the Woodcroft village
sign. However, there is no parking space here, and the view
unfolds less impressively.

The normal **Easy Way Down** on the Central Bay is quicker,
and most convenient for all areas except Go Wall and Fly Wall.
On the left hand side of the road (coming from Tutshill), 500
yards past The Rising Sun and just past the last cottages, is a
small pull-off with space for two or three cars. Starting above
and just left (facing out) of this, descend over easy ledges,
keeping generally in to the right (facing out). Towards the
bottom is a long flat ledge known as the Broadwalk, and from
its far end steps lead down to a path junction. From here: one
track descends straight ahead towards the river to the Wye
Valley path; the north track (right facing out) runs below the
Great Wall and round to the North Wall; the south branch (left
facing out) passes under the Central Bay and meets the Wye
Valley path below the South Bay, whence the remaining
southerly areas can be reached.

A third descent through the **Woodcroft Quarry** (reached
from the road via the lane immediately past Woodcroft Close,
almost opposite The Rising Sun) is most useful for Go Wall and
Fly Wall, though unfortunately the car parking space has
recently been fenced off: the fence was erected to prevent
tipping and to protect local children and should not be further
mutilated. The broad track runs down along the top of Fly Wall
to the head of the scree slope. On the right (facing out) is the
starting ledge of Kama Sutra, Umbrella Girdle, etc.; and left is
the north end of Fly Wall. The scree is highly unstable and
stones dislodged can be dangerous to people on the path below
as well as cause damage to the path itself. If descending to the
foot of Go Wall, do not try to go down the middle of the slope,
but keep to the extreme right margin (facing out) starting
immediately below the arete bounding the upper half of the wall.

The general question of behaviour is most important. The whole
of the climbing area except Fly Wall is situated within the
Lancaut Nature Reserve (see page 84) and most of the top
either lies within, or is very exposed to, private ground.
Woodcroft is not oriented towards tourism and has no interest
in promoting it. Fortunately, the local residents are mostly
friendly and helpful, and relations with them and with the
Nature Reserve Management Committee seem very good at

Introduction

present. However, there have been moves in the past to ban climbing altogether at Wintour's Leap and it is not impossible that such an attempt could succeed. Climbers can help to prevent such an occurrence in the following ways:
Respect the property and privacy of the villagers; keep noise and especially bad language to a minimum near the cliff top.
Refrain from excessive gardening which could threaten wild life: reasonable cleaning of routes in established areas is generally harmless, but avoid wholesale stripping of vegetation or unnecessary trundling.
Observe the Country Code, especially with regard to lighting of fires, damage to hedges and fences, and leaving of litter.
Take care not to dislodge stones on the scree slope (see preceding paragraph).
Regard the Forbidden Wall and the cliffs and woodlands south of this as absolutely out of bounds.
Observe any temporary restriction notices put up by the Nature Reserve Management Committee to protect certain birds in the nesting season (as agreed with B.M.C.). These could occur anywhere, but are most likely on the right half of Go Wall between January and May.
Throughout, the walls and bays and the climbs thereon are described from north to south (left to right). In all cases left and right are as the climber faces the cliff, except where otherwise stated. The word 'right' is used in this context only and never accorded one of its other meanings. 'Corner' means an open book corner, not a square edge, though the name 'Corner Buttress' (Central Bay) has been retained for historical reasons.

Technical

The grading system now becoming standard is used. Each climb is given an adjectival grade which takes account of all factors—those used are:
Moderate, Difficult, Very Difficult, Severe, Hard Severe, Mild Very Severe, Very Severe, Hard Very Severe, Mild Extremely Severe, Extremely Severe
In addition, each pitch of difficulty greater than that normally found on Very Difficult routes is given a numerical grade from 4a to 5c which assesses technical difficulty only, though this is deemed to take into account demands made upon physical strength.

As nut protection is variable and sling belays are almost non-existent except on trees, pegs are necessary here and there. A number are in place: runners are often adequate but several main belays will need augmenting, and climbers are advised to carry a hammer and small selection of pegs on routes above Severe. A medium and small thin blade, one or two Leepers, and two or three angles ($\frac{1}{2}$", $\frac{3}{4}$", and 1"—also on Go Wall a $1\frac{1}{2}$") will cover most contingencies except on artificial pitches. The text generally states where pegs are usually, or might reasonably be, used for protection or main belays, and the introduction to each climb states which are in place at the time of writing (1975/6); though, of course, their continued presence or reliability cannot be assumed. Where a peg is required for aid this is explicitly stated; thus the use of any not so indicated will mean that the pitch has not been climbed at the given standard. Climbers will not need a lecture about over-pegging, but they are entreated not to remove pegs already in place, even if the latter are not considered strictly necessary. Although the limestone is good for occasional pegging the cracks soon wear out, and repeated insertions and extractions can dangerously loosen blocks and holds.

Artificial pitches are graded A1, A2, or A3, and these grades take into account the amount of useful aid in place, which is indicated, along with an estimate of further requirements, in the introduction to the climb; but most of these routes have had so few ascents that it has not been possible to establish standard numbers of aid points. One of the main lines of development now is likely to be the free climbing of some of them, but little progress seems to have been made yet (though see under Interstellar Overdrive and The Umbrella Girdle).

Pitch lengths record the total ground covered from belay to belay, and a few of these are somewhat inflated by ledge-walking. However, to avoid gross distortion where a final belay is well back from the cliff-top, the text sometimes states that the belay is a further number of feet back, and this distance is not then included in the pitch length.

Technical

Some climbs have been given one, two, or three stars to indicate above average quality for the grade. Visitors new to the cliff may find the selection below useful as an introduction. The routes are among the best in their grades, straightforward to reach and follow, and none is at the upper limit of its grade.

Recommended climbs
Difficult Cement Groove ★ (250ft, Central Bay).
Very Difficult Central Rib III ★★★ (230ft, South Bay), Original Route ★ (240ft, Great Wall).
Severe Central Rib I ★★ (225ft, South Bay).
Hard Severe Greta ★★ (190ft, Far South Bay), Left Hand Route ★ (300ft, North Wall), John's Route ★ (205ft, Great Wall).
Mild Very Severe Zelda ★★★ (180ft, Far South Bay), Central Route ★ (350ft, North Wall).
Very Severe The Angel's Girdle ★★★ (360ft, North Wall), Central Rib II ★ (220ft, South Bay), Freedom ★ (110ft, Fly Wall).
Hard Very Severe King Kong ★★★ (300ft, Go Wall), The Angel's Eye ★★ (310ft, North Wall), Puma ★★ (180ft, Far South Bay), Great North Wall Route ★ (300ft, North Wall).
Extremely Severe Kangaroo Wall ★★★ (300ft, Go Wall).
A2 Technician ★★ (340ft, Go Wall).

Historical

Reams could be written about Wintour's Leap by ecologists, geologists, and general historians; but for the climbing chronicler the history, though fairly recent, is obscure and relatively uninspiring. The First Ascent list contains no names of the great pioneers of Wales, Lakeland, or the Peak District, nor of well-known alpinists or Everest climbers. There have been several accidents and a few deaths, but they do not make the headlines and there have been no epic rescues. Climbers have come and gone, perhaps doing a route and often leaving it unrecorded or misrecorded. As has been suggested elsewhere, the cliff has never been taken as seriously as it deserves. Although anonymous members of the Gloucestershire Mountaineering Club and others had climbed here in the 1950s and established such classic easy routes as Central Rib and Original Route, little of importance was done until John Grieve from Cirencester put up Zelda in 1961, following it over the next four years with The Willies, Compost Wall, Gryke, most of Great North Wall Route, Guytha (with alternative start), and The Early Morning Traverse. With protection almost entirely by mild steel pegs (some home-made) in often poor cracks, this is no mean list of achievement.

In the middle of the decade a small group of climbers from Newport became active, notably Terry Broomsgrove and David Dove. A start was made on a complete Lower Wye Valley Guide to replace the old G.M.C. pamphlet; but the pace of development in the area outstripped progress, and with the dispersal of some members of the group to different parts the work fell by the wayside. The Angel's Eye, probably the most popular of the harder climbs, stands as memorial to the partnership. This was done in September 1965, while a few months earlier had appeared the other great classic of the cliff, King Kong, the first breach of Go Wall.

Soon Grieve left for Scotland, but the Severn Bridge was opened and as Bristol climbers took time off from the Gorge the most intensive period of activity began. In the late sixties Fred Bennett paid frequent visits, climbing with his brother Bob, Paul Lennard, and Rob Walker, and there resulted some of the hardest routes at Wintour's Leap: a series of variations on Guytha (hitherto unpublished), and the big Go Wall routes including Kangaroo Wall, Technician, and The Umbrella Girdle. Tony Willmott also came, matching each of these (and employing his well known style of nomenclature) with parallel or eliminate lines of comparable difficulty and quality: Interstallar Overdrive, The Pulsating Rainbow, and The Burning Giraffe.

In the summer of 1967 a party, led apparently by a female of the species (the only one to appear in the First Ascent list),

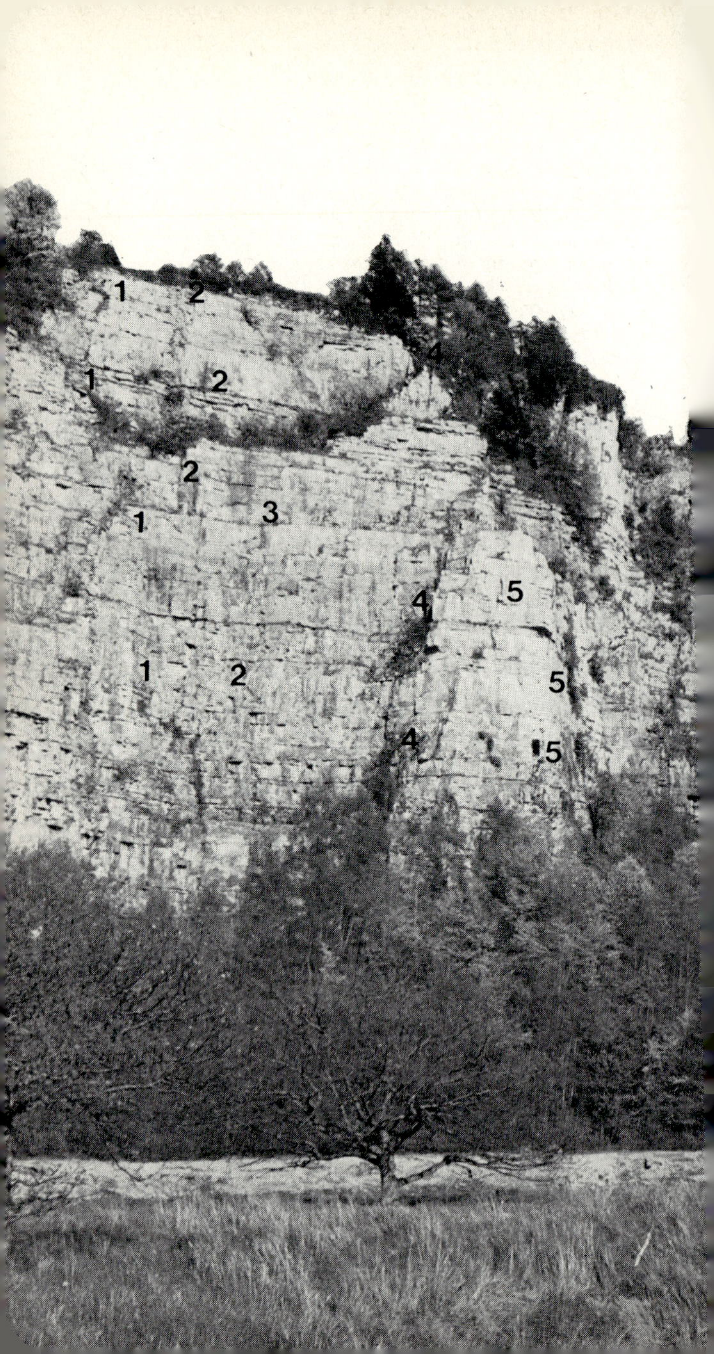
1
2
4
1
2
2
1
3
5
4
1
2
5
4
5

North Wall & Great Wall
1. Left Hand Route
2. Great North Wall Route
3. The Great Ledge
4. Right Hand Route
5. The Angel's Eye
6. Compost Wall
7. John's Route
8. Corner Buttress

Historical

opened up Fly Wall with four bold and difficult routes on the right (longer) half, and within a year all the obvious shorter lines further left were added. But as the decade drew to a close interest petered out. Cannings and Littlejohn did Big Brother in time for Jim Perrin's Interim Guide of 1971, but found more to their liking across the river and further south and west; and Willmott returned in 1972, just before his tragic accident, to complete a unique diagonal traverse on Go Wall started some years earlier: It's A Beautiful Day.

A familiar figure on the scene now, with his dog chasing sticks and stones at the bottom, was Elias (Joe) Fivelsdal, whose climbing debut—in his late forties—was a (truly) solo ascent of Central Rib, and he made Joe's Route (roped solo) in 1973. Over the last few years, he and the author, separately and together, have spent many days working out and rationalising remaining possibilities in the traditional areas of the cliff; and though little of this work is credited in the First Ascent list it is largely responsible for the expansion of this section of the volume.

Though few obvious lines remain, and though the structure of the rock does not always allow the concentration of routes often found elsewhere, there are gaps to be filled in all areas and the time seems ripe for a further, perhaps final, phase of development. A future edition of the guide should certainly be able to include a good number of new routes, as well, one hopes, as to report an improvement in many of the existing ones resulting from the availability of the more comprehensive information contained herein.

The North Wall Area

The North Wall is recessed between the North Buttress on the left and the Angel's Tower on the right, and is split by two large horizontal terraces known as the Main Ledge and the Great Ledge. The lower tier is smooth and vertical with only one line of weakness between its ends; the middle tier is more broken and lies back just a little; the upper tier is heavily vegetated, with some loose rock. The North Buttress is very steep and of variable rock, while the Angel's Tower, also steep, contains the best routes hereabouts and is crossed by the most impressive section of the girdle. Two parallel open corners (Gryke and Left Hand Route) divide the buttress from the wall, the latter being separated from the tower by a shallow wooded gully taken by Right Hand Route.

The way off from the top lies through a small field and private garden: this is not a public right of way but the present owner is co-operative. Please keep out of sight and sound as much as possible. Turn right after crossing the fence and keep close to it; go over a stile (may be replaced by a gate) and pass left of the belvedere. However, climbers are asked not to attempt any finishes left of Left Hand Route. Climbing on the upper tier is mostly unrewarding and some parties prefer to abseil from the Great Ledge. A double 150 foot rope is needed to reach the Main Ledge: if only one rope is available it is necessary to go carefully from tree to tree down Right Hand Route, making sure not to stray rightwards towards Big Brother. The simplest way from the Great Ledge (upon which all the routes converge) to the top (120ft, Moderate—not described under any of the climbs) is to climb blocks in the centre of the wall rightwards then back left, and move left into the forest; walk right up a path and climb a short easy chimney just right of the semi-circular red chimney.

Gryke 310ft Hard Very Severe

The left hand of two parallel open corners between the North Buttress and the North Wall, flanked on the left by a crumbling nose. The climb became mistakenly known as Gripe. Holds are mostly good but rather widely spaced. No pegs are in place except a runner high on pitch 2.

Start (as for Left Hand Route) above the left end of the trough below the wall.

1 60ft. 5a/b. Climb 15 feet to a small ledge. Place a peg below the lower and smaller of two overhangs and use a sling on this for aid. The second overhang goes free: from its top continue, on the right at first, to a stance at the foot of a groove (peg belay).

2 70ft. 4c. Climb the groove (which opens out above) for 50ft to a large ledge on the left. Continue from the right end of the

The North Wall Area

ledge to a higher ledge on the left with a good tree belay.
3 50ft. Climb diagonally right over easier rock to a tree belay on the Great Ledge.
4 130ft. Pitches **3** and **4** of Left Hand Route (Difficult) or **3** and **4** of Great North Wall Route (4b, 4c).

Left Hand Route 300ft Hard Severe ★
Good rock and climbing to the Great Ledge; the upper pitches are more broken and vegetated. Pegs on pitch 2 are in place; that on the first comes and goes.
Start (as for Gryke) above the left end of the trough below the wall.
1 80ft. 4b. Climb 15ft to a small ledge (as for Gryke); move right and then up to the overhang (peg runner). Make a strenuous pull up onto the block on the left. Bear slightly right and continue straight up to a tree and iron spike well above the level of the Main Ledge.
2 90ft. 4a. Climb the wall behind the spike past a peg runner at 10ft and bear left to a niche behind a sapling (peg runner). Mantleshelf onto the left wall and continue straight up for 40ft to a good platform. Move a few feet left to the final overhang, which is climbed using a small sloping red ledge. Tree belays above, though a further 20ft of rope enable a more comfortable belay to be reached on the Great Ledge.
3 60ft. Above the left end of the Great Ledge is a broken, black crystal corner facing right: climb steps on the left of this to a fallen tree. Continue, bearing left at first, over easy but vegetated rock to a cluster of trees.
4 70ft. Move up onto an overhanging block and step right to a short wall; climb this and then more easily up an obvious broken line leaning rightwards to the top (tree belay slightly left).

Variation
Alternative Start 150ft Very Difficult
These two pitches, which include 50ft of ledge walking, provide an easier but less good alternative to pitch 1 only of the direct climb and render the route as a whole Severe.
Start (as for Right Hand Route) in a wooded hollow at the right end of the wall in a large open corner.
1 90ft. Climb up, with a short detour to the right edge at 15ft, to a tree just above the level of the Main Ledge, and traverse left to descend onto the ledge (tree belay near the left-far-end).
2 60ft. Walk 10ft left and climb up bearing left to the tree and iron spike at the foot of pitch 2 of the direct climb.

The Angel's Girdle 360ft Very Severe ★★★
Interesting with good situations all the way, and superbly exposed on pitch 3; there is no ledge walking. All pegs from pitch 2 onwards are in place.
Start as for Left Hand Route.
1 80 feet. 4b. Pitch **1** of Left Hand Route.
2 110ft. 4c. Climb 10ft to the first peg and move right round a bulge to a peg on Central Route. Step up right and traverse horizontally until an awkward move down leads to a peg on Great North Wall Route. Step back up to some easier rightward moves until forced up for 15 feet and round to a sapling. An easier line, but vegetated, now leads past a flake and a gap to a large tree on Right Hand Route.
3 40ft. 4b. Descend a few feet to the top of the crack and follow a line of footholds across the wall to the edge with a peg for aid. Larger holds lead to a peg belay, shared by Big Brother and The Angel's Eye, in a niche in the centre of the tower.
4 130ft. 4c. Reverse the top of pitch **2** of The Angel's Eye as follows: step up and traverse right to the arete; descend this for 20ft until able to move right round to a peg runner at the top of the groove, and make one step down. Step right across the gap (hidden peg runner) and continue horizontally until forced up 10ft at three holes. Traverse right again to join Joe's Route below the short wall with the first fixed peg, and finish up this: climb the wall to a ledge and the next wall on larger holds left of the groovelet to a peg runner; using holds above the overhang, step right across the gap and mantleshelf up short corners to a tree belay below the Great Ledge.
Either continue easily to the Great Ledge and use any of the North Wall finishes; or abseil from the tree belay—150ft of doubled rope nicely reaches the ground. Alternatively, one could continue the traverse by following The Early Morning Traverse in reverse.

Central Route 350ft Mild Very Severe ★
A pleasantly exposed climb with the difficulty well sustained as far as the Great Ledge. Protection is rather sparse in its middle section, which requires careful route finding. Pegs on pitch 2 are in place; that on the first comes and goes.
Start in the trough below the wall at its far left end.
1 80ft. 4b. Climb the left edge until able to swing right into the corner, and move up to a small ledge. Continue to the overhang (peg runner) of Left Hand Route and make a hard move up to a narrow ledge on its right. Step back left on top of the overhang and continue more easily to a grassy area just above the level of the Main Ledge, whence descend onto it.

The North Wall Area

Belay on the first tree at the back of the ledge.
2 80ft. 4b. Starting below the left corner of a rectangular recess, climb up over broken ground, bearing left a little, to a stalactite thread runner. Climb the short steep rib above to an old peg, and then right into a scoop. Move up the scoop until a large step up to the left gives way to an easier diagonally leftward line leading to a stance on top of one overhang and below another (assorted peg and nut belays).
3 60ft. 4b. Traverse 10ft right and climb the steep wall above with a high step up left to a platform. A short corner to the right and a high mantleshelf lead to the Great Ledge. Walk left past the boulder to a tree belay.
4 130ft. Pitches **3** and **4** of Left Hand Route.

Great North Wall Route 300ft Hard Very Severe ★
A fine line with the difficulty well sustained, though not high for the grade. Main belays are good trees, but protection is almost entirely by pegs: those referred to are in place, but further placements may be required.
Start just left of centre of the wall by a bridge across the trough.
1 50ft. 5a. Climb the obvious line of weakness to the Main Ledge.
2 130ft. 5a. From the centre of the ledge, midway between the two largest trees, climb straight up, just right of the rectangular recess, to a peg runner below a tiny overhang, and make a hard move onto the ledge high on the left. Follow a shallow depression, past a peg on the left and another on the right, for 60ft to a short steep corner. Climb this or avoid it by a traverse 5ft right and continue more easily to the Great Ledge. Walk left past the boulder to a tree belay.
3 40ft. 4b. Climb the left-facing crystal corner behind the tree and move right onto a ledge. Climb the short wall on the right to vegetation.
4 80ft. 4c. Climb the steep broken wall above until the angle eases (the rock, though poor, is less bad than it looks).
Traverse steeply left above a tree to a corner of better rock and finish up this.
Note: this route comprises three originally separate climbs. Pitch **1** was called Symplex; **2** was The Tap; **3** and **4** made up Bacchanalian.

The Wrong Tap 300ft Hard Very Severe
A rather mixed route in all respects. Pitch **2** (probably done in mistake for The Tap—see above) is not too well protected and a couple of pegs may be advisable, though not in the loose blocks forming the groove near the top.
Start (as for Right Hand Route) in the wooded hollow below

the right end of the wall in a large open corner.
1 80ft. Climb up (as for Right Hand Route) to a tree just above the level of the Main Ledge, and then traverse left to descend onto it.
2 120ft. 5a. Climb up from the extreme right of the level part of the Main Ledge to a hard move at 40ft onto a small ledge on the right side of a sapling. Step right and continue more easily to a grassy bay, where the pitch could be split. Climb on to a nose, which is taken on its left, and move diagonally right to a groove. Taking great care of the loose blocks forming its right side, climb the groove to easier ground and a tree belay on the Great Ledge.
3 100ft. 4a. Pitches **4** and **5** of Right Hand Route.

Right Hand Route 265ft Severe
Rather a disappointing route: not up to the standard of the rest of the wall.
Start in the wooded hollow at the right end of the wall in a large open corner.
1 50ft. Climb up, with a short detour to the right edge at 15ft, to a tree belay just above the level of the Main Ledge.
2 65ft. 4a. Emerge from the wood behind two large adjacent trees below an overhanging block. Make an awkward move onto this from the left and climb the crack in the wall above in an unexpectedly exposed position. Continue past a large tree to a higher tree belay.
3 50ft. Move up and then right onto easy ledges which lead to the Great Ledge.
4 70ft. High in the wall is a prominent V cleft in the long overhang. Climb up through this to a tree belay below a semi-circular red chimney and a thread on the right.
5 30ft. 4a (plus or minus according to size and shape). Climb the semi-circular chimney facing right. Exit right and step across the shorter chimney to a tree belay. The right hand chimney could of course be climbed instead, thus eliminating both interest and difficulty.

Big Brother 300ft Extremely Severe ★
A bold and technical route on clean rock up the front of the tower. Few of the original pegs are in place, and two additional runners on each of the first two pitches are usually used.
Start in the centre of the tower, 15ft left of The Angel's Eye.
1 80ft. 5b. Climb up and mantleshelf onto a small ledge on the rib on the left and make a hard move to reach a jug (peg runner above). Move left and climb a short groove to the overhang. Traverse 10ft right, climb steeply to better holds, and

The North Wall Area

traverse back left above the overhang. Continue up to a stance and peg belays.
2 50ft. 5c. Climb steeply right for 20ft, move left to the rib, and climb it to good finishing holds: a hard and technical pitch requiring strong fingers. Move right to a peg belay shared with The Angel's Eye in a niche in the centre of the tower.
3 70ft. 4b. Traverse back left to the arete and climb the wall on good holds until easy ledges lead to the Great Ledge.
4 100ft. 4a. Pitches **4** and **5** of Right Hand Route.

The Angel's Eye 310ft Hard Very Severe ★★
The route takes an impressive line up the right edge of the tower and rapidly attained the status of a classic V.S. In recent years, however, a huge block and an aid sling have disappeared from the initial overhangs rendering the start rather fierce. Thereafter the climbing is gentler, though steep, pleasantly exposed, and still with some loose rock and vegetation. Pegs are in place.
Start in the corner at the foot of the arete behind a huge fallen block.
1 80ft. 5a/b. Climb over the overhangs and continue up the groove for 20ft to a peg runner. Make an awkward move right onto the arete and climb this, as its angle relents, back left through vegetation to a peg belay in a cave.
2 80ft. 4b. Traverse diagonally right around the arete to a groove (**not** the diedre which splits the arete itself). Climb the groove to a peg runner and traverse back left to the arete. Climb this on good holds to the overhang, traverse 15ft left, and step down to a peg belay shared with Big Brother in a niche in the centre of the tower.
3 50ft. 4a. Climb the short crack above and continue over easy ledges to the Great Ledge.
4 100ft. 4a. Pitches **4** and **5** of Right Hand Route.

Joe's Route 160ft Very Severe ★
A rather messy start leads to a fine exposed finish on good clean rock. Well protected throughout with pegs in place.
Start in the centre of the south wall of the tower, 15 yards right of The Angel's Eye, in an obvious left-facing corner.
1 60ft. 4a. Climb the corner to a platform with a thin tree. Move up right over a messy band to a stance with large tree belays.
2 100ft. 4c. Step back left onto the rock and climb up past a large tree to a rock spike runner on the floor of a small corner. Step off the spike and traverse diagonally left for 20ft to a short wall split by a thin crack (peg runner) Climb this, and the next wall on larger holds left of the groovelet to a small overhang (peg runner). Using handholds above the overhang, step right

across the gap and mantleshelf up short corners to a tree below the Great Ledge.
Either continue easily to the Great Ledge and reach the top by any of the North Wall finishes; or abseil from the tree belay—150ft of doubled rope nicely reaches the ground.

Narcotic 160ft Very Severe
This could be a worthwhile route, but it badly needs a proper clean up. Nut protection is adequate and pegs are not necessary. Start at the far right end of the extension of the south wall of the Angel's Tower; scramble up to a tree at the foot of a large square corner.
1 80ft. 4b. Move up into the corner and then left to a shallow groove. Climb this and continue on the left wall of the corner to a small overhanging block, at about 40ft, which rocks. Move over this carefully and climb the main corner to a ledge and large tree.
2 25ft. 4c. Move up and left a little, and climb a short crack with an awkward exit onto vegetation and another large tree. Originally the crack in the corner was climbed—rather harder with an even worse exit (two old pegs in place).
3 55ft. 4b. Climb the short borehole crack behind the tree and the wall above. The rock is very bad on the last few feet and there is another exit onto vegetation. Scramble up this to a flat stance and tree belay.
Walk off up to the left, finally emerging at the top of the final chimneys of Right Hand Route.

The Great Wall

Deeply recessed between the Angel's Tower and the Central Bay, and bisected vertically by a prominent rib, the Great Wall is the disappointment of the cliff. It is heavily vegetated (though most of the climbs have been more or less cleaned) and rather less steep than it looks except in some isolated parts. Thus the number of good continuous routes is limited, though there remain some variation and eliminate pitches to be done. However, the three climbs on the right half—The Willies, Original Route, and John's Route—will provide something worthwhile for most. All routes exit onto the road at the top of the cliff.

Compost Wall 170ft Hard Severe
Several of the holds and ledges are sunk deep in earth and compost, and the climb is not recommended in its present condition, though cleaned up it would be a reasonable route and rather easier. Some rusty pegs remain but climbers should be prepared to place their own.
Start on an earthy platform below the left part of the left hand half of the Great Wall, about 100ft above the bottom of the cliff—an obvious path leads up leftwards over grassy ledges.
1 70ft. 4b. Climb diagonally right to a peg a few feet below a gouged-out overhanging block. Move up and onto a ledge left of the block. Continue, bearing right, to a good ledge beneath a V-shaped overhang (peg belay).
2 50ft. 4a. Climb the rib keeping generally on its right side. When able to reach the top block, swing round left to a grass ledge (peg belay).
3 50ft. Move up under the overhang and escape to the right. Easier climbing leads to earth and a gap in the vegetation. Belay on crash barrier.

The Willies 270ft Hard Very Severe
An exciting climb involving bold moves with poor protection (except on the crux) on rock that varies from frightening to excellent. No pegs are in place and one has to get in anything one can.
Start in the centre of the right hand half of the Great Wall, at the foot of a shallow broken groove half way down the slope left of Original Route.
1 90ft. 4c. Climb the groove to a long narrow ledge at the base of the loose band. Traverse horizontally left along this, using rotten handholds, past the open bible. Move up into a depression and step out right onto the top of the left edge of the bible. Make a hard move up to the short groove above and climb it to grass ledges and a peg belay at the foot of the large corner. A sustained pitch of its grade.

2 60ft. 5a (4c if the crux is avoided). Climb the right wall on good but widely spaced holds, bearing slightly right to a gash at its top, just below which is a junction with Original Route. The correct finish is through the gash by means of a hard exposed layback up a huge flake, which does not appear adequately anchored to the cliff. Alternatively, follow Original Route a few feet right and up a short crystal corner onto the ledge. Tree belay in a groove above the far left end of the ledge.
3 120ft. Pitches **3** and **4** of Original Route.

Original Route 240ft Very Difficult ★
A useful route for inexperienced parties, though pitch 3 tends to be muddy and a little loose.
Start at the right hand end of the wall almost at the top of the slope. After descending from the Broadwalk turn right (facing out); a path leads down a little before a fork turns back up to the right (now facing the rock).
1 60ft. Climb steeply up an obvious vertical break to a large ledge. Above, an easier angled scoop bears left to a tree and iron spike.
2 60ft. Follow a diagonal line left, below an eroded groove with a tree, to a slab. Good holds lead up and back right to a short crystal corner, which is climbed to a ledge. Tree belay in a groove above the far left end.
3 70ft. Climb the groove and the left of two very short corners. Continue over muddy ledges, and mantleshelf left onto a large ledge. Tree belay above and just beyond the far left end.
4 50ft. Either: from below the belay climb steeply right and then directly to the top. Or: from the centre of the ledge climb the right edge of the wall on small holds just left of a short roofed groove; continue past an overhang and a large tree to the top. The latter alternative is better, but slightly harder to start.

John's Route 205ft Hard Severe ★
The best and cleanest route on the Great Wall. Protection is good and all pegs are in place.
Start (as for Original Route) at the right hand end of the Great Wall almost at the top of the slope.
1 90ft. 4b. Climb 15ft up the obvious vertical break to the large ledge (as for Original Route) and then two short grooves to the right to a good tree level with the tree and iron spike on Original Route to the left. A line of small holds leads diagonally right across the wall to a peg runner. Make a hard step up; keep to the rock left of the grassy recess and continue to a narrow ledge. Traverse right to a crack: peg and assorted nut belays.
2 90ft. 4b. Climb the crack; pass right of the first overhang to

The Great Wall

a peg runner below the second, which is taken direct. A vegetated band leads to a wall (peg runner), climbed by holds on its left edge with a difficult move at its top. Climb a shorter steeper wall, or the messy corner on its right, to a comfortable stance and peg belay.
3 25ft. Excellent holds lead steeply to the top.

Roger's Route 290ft Very Severe
This route starts on the north facing wall below the Corner Buttress of the Central Bay, and traverses onto the Great Wall. Rather variable in quality, with some bad rock on pitch **4**, it covers a great deal of ground, some of it interesting. Pegs are in place except on pitch **4**.
Start 25ft left of the foot of the steps down from the Broadwalk.
1 80ft. 4a. Scramble up broken blocks to a bent peg runner, and then climb a light-coloured scoop on small holds to a ledge (peg runner). 5ft right a broken line leads, steeply at first, through a gap and then more easily, to a huge ledge and tree.
2 80ft. Walk left and traverse round the large bulge onto the Great Wall, descending slightly to the crack and peg/nut belay at the top of pitch **1** of John's Route.
3 50ft. 4b. Climb the crack, pass right of the first overhang to the peg runner below the second, and take this direct (as for pitch **2** of John's Route). Belay on the next large tree on the right (not the one level with the overhang).
4 80ft. 4c. Traverse right to a rough crack (good peg runner possible), and follow this to the overhanging rib, the side of which is rotten. The short hard wall behind the bush ledge above can be taken in the left corner or further right and leads to easier ground and the top. Belay over the wall.

The Central Bay

This area is ideal for instruction purposes: the rock is generally sound, protection abounds, and the pitches are short and separated by spacious horizontal ledges which connect adjacent routes. It is possible to scramble almost anywhere on the main (west) face except on Black Wall (below the south end of the Broadwalk) and Terry's Wall (the 40ft sandy-coloured wall topping the centre of the bay). Previous guides have described only one or two climbs here, but as a result there is often a queue on Corner Buttress while the rest of the bay is empty. Pegs are nowhere required.

Corner Buttress I and II rise from a corner where the descent from the Broadwalk meets the path. Corner Buttress III, The Problems, Cement Groove, and Black Wall start on the path running south from here below the rock. The remainder except Grey Wall start on the Broadwalk, the long terrace near the bottom of the bay. About 15 feet above it are four prominent silver birch trees, 20 to 25ft apart: these are referred to in the text numbered from the left. All routes (except Black Wall and Grey Wall) exit onto a broad grassy terrace adjacent to the road.

Grey Wall 70ft Very Severe
An interesting pitch, not easy for its grade.
Start 10ft left of the foot of the steps which descend from the Broadwalk.
1 70ft. 4c. Climb pock marks on a short bulging wall to a narrow ledge. The curving crack above, awkward to start, leads to another narrow ledge. Bear left up the final tier to a tree and climb the easy corner on the left to a larger tree. Abseil from here; or escape up Corner Buttress, or to the right and back down onto the Broadwalk.

Corner Buttress Route I 215ft Very Difficult
Start just above the foot of the descent from the Broadwalk, in a short corner.
1 65ft. Climb the corner and two more above, bearing left, to a huge platform and tree.
2 45ft. 4a. Walk right to a crack with a chockstone; climb the overhang to its left, and the next tier by an awkward short groove and ramp (tree belay). (This pitch, though not serious, is technically rather hard for the grade: it can be avoided by following pitch 3 of Corner Buttress III.)
3 55ft. Climb the twin cracks behind the tree. Continue to the foot of the buttress and climb the rough crack, left of centre, past a small tree to a good platform and tree belay.
4 50ft. Climb the easy left edge to the top (nut belay, or a tree a further 25ft back).

The Central Bay

Corner Buttress Route II 215ft Very Difficult
Start (as for Corner Buttress I) just above the foot of the descent from the Broadwalk, in a short corner.
1 70ft. Climb the right walls of the first two corners by their edges to a tree. Climb the tree and/or the wall behind it to a large ledge (chockstone belay in the crack).
2 30ft. 4a. Climb the crack, and a second, thinner one to the right in the tier above (tree belay). (As with pitch **2** of the preceding route, this can be avoided by following pitch **3** of Corner Buttress III.)
3 70ft. Take the slab right of the tree; move on to the foot of the steep right edge of the buttress and climb this to the large platform and tree belay. (Unless endowed with a long reach it is easier to start a few feet right of the arête and traverse back in just above.)
4 45ft. Continue easily to the top keeping right (nut belay, or a tree a further 25ft back).

Corner Buttress Route III 275ft Moderate
The easiest route on the cliff.
Start on the path below the bay, 10 yards south of the junction at the foot of the descent from the Broadwalk.
1 90ft. Climb 45ft to a tree just below the left end of the Broadwalk (the pitch could be split here). Take an easy line diagonally right to the first silver birch.
2 40ft. Climb the short open corner above and left of the tree. Walk left to a crack with a chockstone to belay.
3 40ft. Climb right of the crack, walk left round the short arête, and scramble up the next tier to a tree belay.
4 55ft. Move up and climb the broken left edge of the buttress on enormous holds to a good platform and tree.
5 50ft. Continue to the top on large holds to the left (nut belay, or a tree a further 25ft back).

The Problems
A series of interesting moves and very short pitches separated by scrambling. Competent climbers solo them, while less experienced parties will find it easy to by-pass each to fix a top rope. An over-all grade would be inappropriate, but the numerical gradings give a handy guide to standards found elsewhere on the cliff.
Start on the path below the bay, 20 yards south of the junction at the foot of the descent from the Broadwalk, beneath a small overhang.
1 4a. Climb the overhang direct; continue past the boulder ledge to the Broadwalk.
2 4a. Below and 8ft left of the second silver birch is a short

crack with a hole at 6ft.
3 4c. Behind the tree and 2ft left, tiny holds lead to a curving crack and better holds.
4 5a. Traverse left until forced up a short corner to a large ledge: the far left edge is a 15ft vertical arête.
5 4b. Traverse diagonally right to a prominent overhang on the right hand face of the buttress and climb over its centre. Move left to a large platform and tree.
6 4b. Climb the centres of the two short walls above, avoiding holds to left and right.

Cement Groove 250ft Difficult ★
The best climb in the bay and quite good for its grade.
Start (as for The Problems) on the path below the bay, 20 yards south of the junction at the foot of the descent from the Broadwalk
1 60ft. Climb up just right of the overhang, and on past the boulder ledge to the Broadwalk (bush belay).
2 60ft. Above the left end of the Broadwalk is a short shallow groove which looks as if its back has been plastered with cement. Climb this to a large ledge (chockstone belay in the crack ahead).
3 85ft. From the extreme right end of the ledge step up and traverse diagonally right below two groove-backed alcoves. Enter the second (larger) one from its right, climb diagonally right onto a ridge, and continue up this to a tree.
4 45ft. Climb steeply behind the tree to grass ledges and finish up the eroded groove in the rib above, which separates the Corner Buttress from the gully to its right. Nut belay, or a tree a further 25ft back.

Black Wall 50ft Very Severe
Steep and rather strenuous with some suspect rock.
Start on the path below the bay, 35 yards south of the junction below the foot of the descent from the Broadwalk: the black wall 8ft left of a corner.
1 50ft. 4b. Climb up behind a tree to a gash. Keep this on the right and bear left to a hard move up, followed by easier ground for 10ft to the Broadwalk.

Direct Route 155ft Difficult
Start on the Broadwalk below the second silver birch.
1 50ft. Climb the wall above and right of the tree. Move right up the next tier and back left to a small tree.
2 50ft. Climb behind the tree: harder at first until jugs are reached. Continue over a broken band—to left or right—to a large alcove with trees.

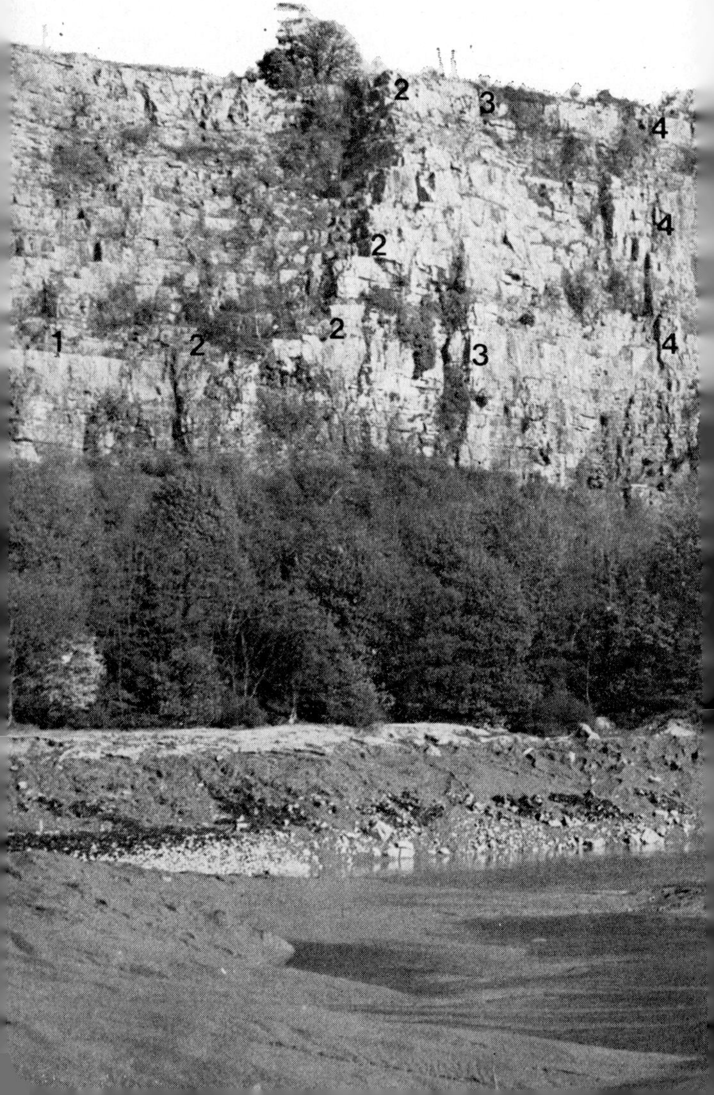
2
3
4
4
2
1
2
2
3
4

**Central Bay, South Bay,
Far South Bay, Go Wall**
1 The Broadwalk
2 Easy Way Down
3 Bottle Buttress
4 The Central Rib
5 The Deceiver
6 The Ragged Edge
7 King Kong
8 The Umbrella Girdle
9 The Burning Giraffe

The Central Bay

3 55ft. Scramble up the gully to the left and back right to a short vertical wall, and climb this to the top. Tree belay a further 20ft back.

Variation
Direct Finish 55ft Very Difficult
3a 55ft. Climb the steep broken rock immediately behind the trees to easier ground (unpleasant when muddy). Bear left to the same final wall.

Centre Route 150ft Severe
Low in its grade and of no special interest.
Start on the Broadwalk below the third silver birch.
1 70ft. Climb the short corner behind the tree. Continue straight up over easy ground to a solitary tree almost level with the forest on the right.
2 40ft. Climb on over short walls and ledges to a grass ledge at the base of Terry's Wall. Belay on the left hand tree.
3 40ft. 4a. Climb the broken line, starting in the centre of the wall and bearing left a little.

Variation
Right Hand Finish 40ft Hard Severe
3a 40ft. 4b. Rather better: from the right hand tree, climb past a small circular hole giving a good thread, and over a shallow overhang. A step left is necessary; then climb straight to the top.

Ridge By-Pass 200ft Moderate
Start (as for Ridge Route) on the Broadwalk below the third silver birch.
1 45ft. (As for Ridge Route) scramble to the tree and on right of the corner to a ledge and tree belay.
2 45ft. Climb straight over the next two tiers by an easy line 10ft left of the short chimney. Tree belay on the edge of the forest.
3 70ft. Move in a semi-circle round the left edge of the forest and climb diagonally right over ledges to a tree on a small platform in a short corner.
4 40ft. Step up onto the ridge, and continue, finishing up the short scoop (tree belay a further 20ft back).

Ridge Route 185ft Moderate
A good route for novices.
Start on the Broadwalk below the third silver birch.
1 45ft. Scramble to the tree and on right of the corner to a ledge and tree belay.
2 50ft. Climb a short chimney on the right; step back left and

climb a steep vertical break in the next tier. Continue easily to a tree on the edge of the forest.
3 40ft. Walk right to the foot of the ridge and climb it to a bush belay on the right.
4 50ft. Continue up the ridge, which fades into a scoop just below the top: exit via this (tree belay a further 20ft back).

Wye Knot 180ft Difficult
Start at the right end of the Broadwalk.
1 60ft. Scramble up right to the fourth silver birch. Zig-zag left up a ramp and back right to a large tree on a small ledge.
2 70ft. Make a difficult move up the wall behind the tree and traverse diagonally right across the foot of the ridge to a bush.
3 50ft. Climb the broken wall on the right of the ridge to the top. The rock looks bad but is quite safe if handled sensibly. Tree belay a further 20ft back.

Climbing on short sections further right is possible but there is no continuity. A small buttress at the top of the cliff is worthwhile.

The South Bay

Broad, shallow, and open to the sun, this bay is the most popular area of the cliff and contains a variety of good climbs in the lower and middle grades, most of them relatively free from vegetation, bad rock, and serious situations. There are three main routes each with its own network of variants. Bottle Buttress is on the left, and the Central Rib tumbles steeply down the middle of the bay. Further right, where the bay merges with Deceiver Buttress, the cliff lies back and is broken by many ledges, giving an easy line with some harder direct finishes.

The climbs, except for Prang, This, and That, all start from a ledge system 20 to 30ft above the bottom, which is reached by a simple scramble. Take the obvious track which leads up from the main path for the central and right hand routes, and the left branch just below the rock for the Bottle Buttress climbs. This and That start half way up the Beginner's Route at the bottom right hand corner of a prominent vertical black wall; a more interesting approach is to climb the first pitch of one of the Central Rib routes and then traverse horizontally right. All climbs exit onto or just in front of Offa's Dyke footpath.

Prang 225ft Hard Very Severe
The grade is barely warranted. A good protection peg on the crux of pitch **1** would reduce it to V.S.
Start at ground level at a short obvious groove 15ft left of the left end of the ledge system.
1 70ft. 5a. Climb the groove to the bramble ledge. Take a direct line up the wall past a peg runner to a protruding hold in the horizontal fault. Continue straight up to a hard finishing move just below the tree belay on pitch **1** of Bottle Buttress.
2 55ft. 4b. Scramble 15ft diagonally right to a larger ledge and tree. Climb the half-formed crack behind the tree with finger holes and a thread runner. Continue easily to the fallen block and two trees.
3 100ft. 4b. Left of the belays and right of a semi-circular overhang is a short steep crack. Climb this and the tapering slab above. Traverse diagonally left below a steep wall to a dirty crack at its far end, which is used to gain better holds on the right on the wall. Easy grass and rubble leads to a good tree below the top.

Bottle Buttress 270ft Very Difficult ★
A rather wayward route, but with some interesting moves. A second coming off on either of the last two pitches could take an unpleasant swing.
Start left of a bush at the left end of the ledge system that runs

along the bay 20ft above the ground.

1 50ft. Make an awkward pull up to the left across the slab, or move up by the bush and then left. Climb through a gap in the overhang and continue, bearing left, to a short corner with a tree belay at its top. This is not the tree on the wall to the right which is visible from the foot of the climb.

2 80ft. Climb easily diagonally right to a ledge and tree. Step up behind the tree, traverse right for 15ft on small holds above the level of the ledge, and climb a scoop on sloping holds to another ledge. The broken wall a few feet left leads to a fallen block and two trees.

3 140ft. Move left onto and along a sloping ramp to a corner (old peg runner in place): a hidden undercut well forward assists an awkward move past the gap. An easier alternative is to descend a few feet left from the belay and gain the ramp beyond the gap. Step out left of the corner and continue straight up an obvious line, which relents all the while, to easy ground just below the top: plenty of cracks for sound nut belays. If only a 120ft rope is used, from 30ft above the corner peg traverse horizontally left on a narrow grass ledge and round the arête to a large platform beside the Easy Way Down with nut and chockstone belays (90ft). Make a way to the top to taste.

Bottle Buttress Direct 210ft Very Severe ★
A rather artificial line, its name being justified only in relation to the ordinary route, which meanders even more; but well worth doing for a variety of interesting and strenuous moves. The peg, which is in place, has been used since the disappearance of loose jugs.

Start 15ft right of the bush at the foot of the ordinary route (which is at the far left end of the ledge system 20ft above the ground) on a small block ledge above the main ledge.

1 70ft. 4c. Using a crack on the right, climb steeply up to a small ledge at 20ft, and move left to a peg, which is used to aid a hard pull-up to the left. With a short detour left and back, move up into a corner, and climb this until level with a prominent tree on the left. Traverse to the tree; then climb the vague riblet, bearing slightly right, to a ledge and tree.

2 40ft. 4b. Here Prang is joined and followed to the top: behind the tree is a half-formed crack with finger holes and a thread runner which leads to a ledge; continue easily to the fallen block and two trees.

3 100ft. 4b. Pitch **3** of Prang.

Broken Bottle 280ft Very Severe A1
A good introduction to artificial climbing. About six pegs are

The South Bay

required: a couple of blades extra to the standard selection will suffice and a small nut is useful.
Start behind a large bush on the ledge system, midway between Bottle Buttress and Central Rib, below a shallow groove which indents the upper of two small overhangs.

1 60ft. 4b + A1. Free climb to the first overhang. Peg over the overhangs and traverse right (free) below a borehole into a small corner (peg belay).

2 80ft. 4b. Traverse back left on good holds, past the line of pitch **1,** until forced to make a hard move up left to a dark scoop. Climb this or the lighter coloured one on its left to a ledge, and then easily to the fallen block and two trees on Bottle Buttress. A difficult pitch to protect.

3 140ft. 4a. Climb the steep flake crack above and right of the belay. Make a further move above the flake and then a long horizontal traverse left to a sapling on Bottle Buttress. Climb straight up easily to broken ground below the top: plenty of cracks for sound nut belays.

Central Rib Route I 225ft Severe ★★

The best route of its grade on the cliff.
Start on the large platform below and left of the rib, 20ft above the ground.

1 85ft. Climb the centre of the wall above for 20ft, and then bear right to a ledge beside the rib (old peg runner in a short borehole crack). As for Central Rib III, climb the groove to a small ledge and then bear left to a large tree at the foot of the long corner.

2 40ft. 4a. Climb the corner to the remains of a small tree a little above the ledge at its top.

3 50ft. From the belay walk 10ft left and then climb diagonally right back to the rib. Move up left of a small nose to the forest platform.

4 50ft. 4a. Scramble to the next ledge and climb the final steep wall on small but adequate holds, starting in the centre below and just right of the small ledge at half height. An easier alternative for those endowed with a long reach is the borehole crack at the left end of the wall.

Central Rib Route II 220ft Very Severe ★

A good technical route: the situation is not serious for the grade, but there are some committing moves which can seem hard if the correct sequence is not found. Belay peg is in place but a runner is advisable on pitch **1.**
Start (as for Central Rib I) on the large platform below and left of the rib, 20ft above the ground.

1 90ft. 4c. Bridge up the corner formed by the rib and its left wall, and move out onto the rib, which is climbed direct. There are good peg runner cracks below the steep section: take this near the left edge at first, and then move right past a large crystal hole in the loose band. A final awkward move up leads to a platform and peg belay.

2 70ft. 4b. Climb the left arête of the rib to a platform. Hand traverse left across the top of the long corner and move round into a shorter corner. Climb this and then the steep crack splitting the centre of the wall above (tree belay just below the forest).

3 60ft. 4c. Move up left of the trees to the long ledge. The final wall is climbed on very small holds on the right to a gash at its top.

Central Rib Route III 230ft Very Difficult ★★★
A classic, and as fine a route of its grade as is likely to be found on British limestone.
Start (as for the other Central Rib Routes) on the large platform below and left of the rib, 20ft above the ground.

1 90ft. Scramble to the foot of the rib, and climb it for 40ft to a small ledge on the left (old peg runner in a short borehole crack). Climb the groove—useful right holds on the rib—to a small ledge and then bear left to a large tree at the foot of the long corner. This section can be quite hard if wet—an inferior detour is possible from the peg round to the right of the rib.

2 50ft. Traverse right to a platform and climb the crest of the rib, steeply at first, to another platform (belay on remains of a small tree above this).

3 40ft. Continue straight up through a gap between a small nose on the left and an overhanging block on the right to the forest platform.

4 50ft. Scramble diagonally right past vegetation to a small buttress of clean rock in a fine position. An obvious broken line leads up the front of this to the top.

This 85ft Very Severe
Short, but steep and strenuous all the way except for one resting ledge. Holds are always adequate, but sometimes dirty. Not easy for the grade. Pegs are not required.
Start half way up the Beginner's Route, at the bottom right hand corner of the large black wall, at the foot of an obvious groove topped by a winding crack. Good tree belay 10ft below and left.

1 85ft. 4c. Bridge up the groove to a grass ledge at its top on the right. Move up and slightly left to gain a good pocket for the left fist. Climb directly up to the foot of the flake crack and follow this to the top.

The South Bay

That 105ft Severe
A useful short route.
Start half way up the Beginner's Route, 6ft right of the groove of This, beneath a small overhang on the left edge of the buttress.
1 45ft. 4a. Climb straight up to a comfortable platform and belay on the higher of two trees: steep and somewhat blind, but good holds always materialise.
2 60ft. 4a. Climb over earth and grass ledges a few feet right to a shallow red chimney, and follow this, finishing slightly right.

The Beginner's Route 260ft Moderate
A safe training route. Numerous variations are possible until the final tree, and the pitches can be split or re-arranged ad lib. with plenty of sound tree belays.
Start (as for the Central Rib routes) on the large platform below and left of the rib, 20ft above the ground.
1 110ft. Traverse right over vegetated ledges past the foot of the rib. Climb a vague area of broken rock picking a line to taste—generally easier to the right—to a ledge and tree.
2 120ft. Climb to the next tree and up a short open corner behind it. Now take a diagonal line to the very large tree on the right skyline 30ft below the top. The final few feet to the tree are steep and often muddy, but holds are enormous. Belay on a branch.
3 30ft. Step right and climb broken rock to the top (block belay or a tree a further 15ft back).

Deceiver Buttress South Buttress

Separating the South and Far South Bays is a 150ft high church-door shaped buttress composed of some of the worst rock at Wintour's Leap. Above its apex the bays merge to form a broad easy-angled ridge taken by the final section of The Beginner's Route. At present there is only one complete route in use (but see Appendix for miscellanea) and, wisely perhaps, no-one appears to have tried going straight over the long roof.

The Deceiver 200ft Mild Extremely Severe
A committing climb on some dangerous rock. Peg and nut protection is not difficult to arrange but may be unreliable, though main belays are adequate.
Start left of centre of the buttress, below a semi-circular overhang which tops a very short rib, flanked on either side by an equally short groove.
1 60ft. 5a. Climb up onto the left side of the rib and move round into the right groove; go up and escape right of the overhang. Follow a long crack, with a sling for aid to start, until forced right by a small overhang. Climb a short corner to a strenuous move up right onto a flat ledge (peg belays). The aid point (peg unnecessary—tape knot sits in crack) was not mentioned in the 1971 guide, but was used on the first ascent and is not known to have been dispensed with.
2 140ft. 5b. Move up above the belay over a small loose overhang; climb a steep shallow groove and exit right. Traverse left along a narrow ledge and climb a short corner. Now take the line of least resistance diagonally left to by-pass the left end of the long roof. Climb the smooth final wall past an old peg to a ledge; then continue easily to a tree on a large platform. Scrambling leads to the top of the cliff.

The Far South Bay

This is the concave area between Deceiver Buttress and Go Wall. The lower 150ft is uniformly steep and unspoilt by the usual large ledges. Unfortunately, the upper 50ft lies right back, is heavily vegetated, and collects locals' rubbish. All the climbs (except The Ragged Edge, which traverses out onto Go Wall) finish below this, and escape is by a scramble up left to the top of the Beginner's Route, which exits onto Offa's Dyke footpath. All the routes (four of which, hitherto unpublished, have had only a handful of ascents) are high quality climbs, free of any aid, on good clean rock. Steep, sustained, and exposed, they deserve the attention of all competent parties. Nut protection is variable, but there are generally good peg cracks where nothing else is possible. Cobra, Puma, and The Ragged Edge are variation finishes to Guytha. No details of these three were available apart from their relative positions, and they were climbed for this write-up by guesswork. It is possible that they could take more direct or independent lines.

Greta 190ft Hard Severe ★★
A good route with a much improved finish. Peg runners are in place, but a second is advisable on pitch **2**; main belays need augmenting.
Start in a large pit, below and left of the prominent corner of Zelda.
1 60ft. 4a. Climb the slab, bearing left, to a narrow ledge; traverse to its left end and climb the corner past a peg runner to a peg belay in a niche.
2 70ft. 4b. Bridge out over the niche to a peg runner. Climb diagonally right past a small bulge to a narrow ledge (peg crack—last good protection on this pitch) and move up until level with some loose flakes on the right. Traverse a few feet left and climb the middle of the depression above to hidden jugs. Bear right past a sapling to a peg belay in the red band at the top of pitch **2** of Zelda.
3 60ft. 4a. Move left to a short wall and climb this behind a sapling in its centre, or more easily behind the tree further left, to a sloping grass platform. Climb a pillar on the right past a second, smaller grass platform, to a hidden peg runner at its top, and make an awkward step right round the bulge. Move up easily for 10ft, and then either traverse right to the final ledge and tree of Zelda, or continue up to a stance and place a peg. In either case, scramble up left to the top.

The Early Morning Traverse 1500ft Mild Very Severe
More of an outing than a climb, demanding resourcefulness in route-finding on vegetated ledges rather than a neat techique. Little of the route is above severe standard and much of it is

below. However, hammer and pegs should be carried, and a double 150ft rope is necessary. Well worthwhile for anyone who likes this sort of thing.

Start as for Zelda.

01 115ft. 4b. Pitches **1** and **2** of Zelda (or, equally well, **1** and **2** of Greta).

02 120ft. From the peg belay in the red band, move left past vegetation and a tree, and follow a rising line onto a huge platform. From its upper level, go round the edge and descend 5ft by an iron spike. Tree belay on the same ledge.

03 80ft. Walk left and descend 15ft; climb back up in the earthy, shallow corner formed by the Central Rib and the wall to its right. From a platform, step down and round to the left to the tree belay at the foot of the long corner crack on Central Rib.

04 65ft. Traverse horizontally left past a large tree to the fallen block and two trees at the top of pitch **2** of the Bottle Buttress routes.

05 130ft. 4a. Climb the flake crack on the right; make a further step up and then a long horizontal traverse left to a sapling on Bottle Buttress (as for Broken Bottle pitch **3**). Descend 10ft from the sapling and move round the edge to a platform on the Easy Way Down: nut belays.

06 100ft. An easy pitch, horizontally for 50ft over grass and rubbish, and then diagonally up to a bush belay on the side of the Ridge.

07 120ft. Continue diagonally to the grass ledge at the base of Terry's Wall; then make a long horizontal traverse, passing just above the alcove on Direct Route, to the platform and tree on Corner Buttress below the top pitch of its climbs.

08 85ft. Descend the easy left edge of the buttress, cross a rubbish bay in the broadest part of the gully, and continue, ascending slightly, to a belay half way up a tall tree standing in a corner.

09 120ft. 4a. Continue the gently rising line over bad rock to John's Route. Step up and follow an obvious, but narrow and mainly grass, ledge horizontally all the way to the large ledge below the last pitch of Original Route (tree belay above the far left end).

10 90ft. 4a. Walk left behind the trees and move up 5ft. Traverse horizontally and cross a corner to a peg on the edge. Abseil 30ft down to the left to a vegetated ledge on the wall (peg belay). This manoeuvre requires careful and competent execution. The peg belay—which must then be used for the next abseil—is not in place; and a second is also advisable to back up the ancient first abseil peg. These can be retrieved later by abseiling from the large tree at the top of the cliff—150ft of

The Far South Bay

rope will reach easy ground at the bottom.

11 100ft. Abseil again to the foot of the wall. It is possible to eliminate this abseil by crossing the wall at various points, but all at a higher standard than anything else on the route, and involving an awkward descent on dangerous ground the other side.

12 75ft. Walk left along the base of the wall and scramble up and round to a block belay in a cave.

13 110ft. 4a. Traverse left, easily at first across a wide grassy gully, gaining a little height. Cross the corner onto the opposite wall (more exposed now), and make an awkward 10ft descent to a large tree level with the Great Ledge further left. This is the belay at the top of pitch **2** of Narcotic and should not be confused with the one 20ft lower and a little to the right.

14 90ft. 4b. Climb back up the borehole crack behind the tree and move left to the edge. Step down to a tiny platform and hand traverse round and along to easy ground. Continue to a tree belay on the Great Ledge.

15 100ft. 4a. Pitches **4** and **5** of Right Hand Route.

Zelda 180ft Mild Very Severe ★★★
A very fine climb with some bold exposed moves. Peg runners are in place, though a second may be required on pitch **3** and main belays need augmenting.
Start at the foot of a steep right-facing corner in the centre of the bay; an earthy ridge leads up.

1 60ft. 4b. Climb the corner for 30ft until level with a peg runner on the left wall. Traverse left to the arête and make a hard move up. Easier ground leads to a small stance and peg belay.

2 55ft. 4a. An obvious line leads steeply leftward past a small tree to a peg belay on the edge in the red band.

3 65ft. 4b. Step up and traverse horizontally right to a peg runner. Move onto and round the nose, and then up, bearing left, to a small ledge at the base of a sentry box. Bridge up over this and climb a short open corner to a large platform and tree belay.

Scramble up left to the top.

Cobra 170ft Hard Very Severe ★
Provides a short, vicious finish in place of the less hard, but very exposed finish of Puma. Peg required for main belay and one for protection on pitch **2**.
Start as for Guytha.

1 60ft. 5a. Guytha pitch **1**, or **1a** (90ft-4b).

2 75ft. 4c. Follow Guytha for 30ft: make a difficult move up

from the left of the ledge keeping clear of the hanging flake, move back right into the groove and follow the gully. From a short borehole just below the bush, traverse 15ft left and climb broken blocks to an alcove with a small ash.
3 35ft. 5b. A gently overhanging flake crack curves round to the left: the rock appears to be quite sound. Climb the crack to the platform and tree at the top of Zelda.
Scramble up left to the top.

Puma 180ft Hard Very Severe ★★
This variant makes the best route of the quartet, with a superbly exposed finish. Two pegs will be required for protection, one on each of the last two pitches, and one for the main belay.
Start as for Guytha.
1 60ft. 5a. Guytha pitch **1,** or **1a** (90ft-4b).
2 75ft. 4c. Cobra pitch **2.**
3 45ft. 4c. Step up and traverse right, placing a peg runner, past a tiny platform to the rib, which is climbed to its top. Easy ledges on the right lead to a large platform and good nut belays in a long slab crack.
Scramble up left to the top.

Guytha (**South Gully**) 160ft Hard Very Severe ★
A straightforward line on mainly good rock. Two pegs are required for protection on pitch **2** and one for the main belay.
Start at the highest point in the centre of the bay, 10ft right of the large corner of Zelda.
1 60ft. 5a. Step up left onto a small shelf. Make a very thin traverse right to gain a good handhold and move straight on up over dubious rock until the angle relents. Continue more easily, passing left of a peg runner under a small overhang, to a turf platform below the initials R.B. (peg belay).
2 100ft. 5a. Make a difficult move up from the left of the ledge keeping clear of the hanging flake and move back right into the groove. Follow the gully, passing left of the bush, to two large trees at its top. The final groove involves very smooth bridging and should be protected by a good peg.
Traverse horizontally left for 30ft on grass and rubbish ledges and then scramble up left to the top.

Variation
Alternative Start 90ft Mild Very Severe
Start as for Zelda.
1a 90ft. 4b. Climb pitch **1** of Zelda, and then traverse 30ft diagonally right to the same turf ledge.

The Far South Bay

The Ragged Edge 280ft Hard Very Severe
Starting in the Far South Bay, this traverses out right onto the edge dividing the bay from Go Wall: interesting climbing with attractive situations, if less sensational than those of the Go Wall routes proper. There is some loose rock and vegetation, but it occurs mostly on the easier sections and does not affect the seriousness of the route.
Start (as for Guytha) at the highest point in the centre of the bay, 10ft right of the large corner of Zelda.
1 70ft. 5a. Follow Guytha for 30ft: step up left onto a small shelf; make a very thin traverse right to gain a good handhold and move straight on up over dubious rock until the angle relents. Traverse right on grass ledges to a corner and go up to a tree.
2 65ft. 5b. Continue up the corner, passing right of bushes, to a niche below white patches underneath an overhang. Climb straight up to the overhang (peg runner in place) and over it. Continue past a small tree to a larger one in the corner (belay shared with Umbrella Girdle).
3 45ft. 4c. Move up and traverse right to the obvious crack which detaches the enormous perched flake. Climb the crack to a platform and on up near the edge to the next platform (vast array of belay possibilities).
4 80ft. 4b. Climb the rib above on excellent holds. Go up over grass between trees and move left; mantleshelf into a spacious alcove (tree belay).
5 20ft. 4a. Climb the steep wall left of the loose crack to the top.

Go Wall

The Great Overhanging Wall is probably the finest piece of inland rock in southern England, apart from Cheddar, and also one of the most serious. In places in the middle of the wall rescue, retreat, or escape could be an extremely difficult operation. Route finding is generally not a problem, but the artificial climbs especially are prodigiously time consuming, and one should always allow a generous margin of time, competence, and equipment (including prusikers or loops). Despite the trees at the bottom and the wooded top terrace, the situations are magnificent and the climbing is always varied and interesting.

Seagulls often nest around the level of The Burning Giraffe, especially in the cave on Kangaroo, and can be troublesome. Ravens also sometimes nest on the wall, and as they are protected birds some restrictions on climbing may be necessary here during the nesting season between January and May. Please observe any temporary restriction notices placed by the Nature Reserve Management Committee: these are kept to a minimum and their disregard could lead to more stringent control.

The last five climbs in this section, The Umbrella Girdle, Parasol, It's A Beautiful Day, The Burning Giraffe, and Kama Sutra, start half way up the wall from a ledge which leads in from the right from the top of the scree slope; all others begin along the bottom. The final chimney of King Kong, on which many of the routes converge, emerges in the woods behind Offa's Dyke footpath, while the rightmost climbs finish in an extension to the garden of the house across the path. The owner kindly allows climbers to cross this, but please do not use it for camping or other purposes.

Kaiser Wall 360ft Very Severe A2

The wall, though very steep, is less overhanging here than further right and the rock is less good, especially on the first pitch. The main interest is concentrated in the aid placements. Allow a very long day and take a large and varied selection of pegs as well as a bathook.

Start 20ft in from the left of Go Wall, midway between the latter and King Kong, at a short vertical break.

1 80ft. 4a + A2. Reach a fixed peg in the break and peg up a thin vertical crack for 15ft. Traverse 10ft right and climb straight up on poor pegs to a bolt below the small roof. Go over the roof with a bathook in an invisible bolt hole immediately above, and continue onto the top of the higher overhang slightly left. A short free section and some sounder pegs lead back slightly right to the large tree.

2 40ft. 4a + A1. Climb the crack on the right behind the tree

Go Wall

on good pegs (or nuts). The last 15ft are free: step right and climb a small groove to the main ledge (thread and peg belays slightly right).

3 80ft. 4b + A2. Peg straight up to a bolt at 20ft. Make two free steps left and peg up to the next overhang, which appears to expand. Round its left edge is a long thin groove: continue up this on pegs for 15ft to a very narrow ledge. Traverse left along this to a good stance and tree belay. However, it ought to be possible to go straight on up the groove to a higher horizontal fault, and then move left into the recess.

4 130ft. 4b. Move up to the next ledge; climb the recess, taking care of bad rock, and exit right. Walk a long way right through the trees to a short open groove.

5 30ft. 4a. Climb the groove, or the final pitch of King Kong which is just to the right.

King Kong 300ft Hard Very Severe ★★★

A climb of great character, with good protection on the hardest moves. A wedge-shaped block is easing itself out 15ft up and this could affect the standard of the start. Sufficient pegs are in place.

Start 40ft in from the left end of the wall beneath a prominent overhang; above this an obvious groove line goes right up the cliff.

1 140ft. 5a/b. Climb up to and over the overhang on its left to a small ledge. This point can be reached more easily by a diagonal line from a start 10ft to the right. Follow the corner above until just below the roof and traverse right onto the rib. Move up and back into the groove and continue more easily for 50ft. Traverse right across a wall at half height to the arête, bear left up a short slab, and bridge and layback up the corner starting in the right hand crack before moving to the left. Various belays in the corner behind the tree.

2 130ft. 4c. Climb the corner, taking care with the semi-detached flakes. Move left beneath the overhang (peg runner) and pull over it into the groove above. Climb this and then vegetation to thread belays below a corner chimney.

3 30ft. 4a. Climb the chimney, moving onto the left wall—or the wall all the way—to a good tree belay at the top.

Interstellar Overdrive 330ft Hard Very Severe A2

An eliminate line with the peg pitch pleasantly situated. Willmott is reported to have done this mainly (?) free before his death, but no confirmation or details are available and the route is described as usually done. The pitch is less complicated than it sounds and a few fixed pegs help show the way. Take a varied selection of pegs including a $2\frac{1}{2}$" bong.

Start 20ft right of King Kong below an overhanging groove.
1 140ft. 5b. Climb 10ft and mantleshelf onto a ledge in the bottom of the groove. Climb the groove and exit left at the top. Move right to a small cave, right again, and then up right with a peg (in place) for aid. Hand traverse right to a peg runner and pull over the overhang above to a ledge. Move up right to join Kangaroo Wall and continue up to the base of the crack. Traverse left along the highest root ledge and step around the nose to a loose ramp. Follow this to the stance and peg belay of Kangaroo.
2 80ft. A2. Climb free up to the overhangs and move left to a shallow groove. Peg over the bulge and up the corner. Go right and then left round the next roof to a minute corner. Go right between roofs and climb the last one over its right hand side into a long shallow groove. Climb this until able to move up right to the cave on Kangaroo Wall (peg belay). Care should be taken to avoid rope drag as the last 10ft are free anyway.
3 110ft. 5a or 4c. Pitches **3** and **4** of Kangaroo Wall.
The 1971 guide mentioned the possible existence of an independent finish. No-one seems to know about this but the following *looks* possible, and not too hard: continue straight up the final groove of pitch **2** to the horizontal fault. Traverse left along this past a tree to a large corner in the arête and belay. Move up and then out left to join the final few feet of rock and the vegetation at the top of pitch **2** of King Kong and finish up that climb.

Kangaroo Wall 300ft Extremely Severe ★★★
This must lay claim to being the finest route on the cliff, if not in the whole Wye Valley: a superb natural line, less transparent than King Kong, giving good sustained climbing in magnificent situations. The rock is clean except for a short bit in the middle of the first pitch and the inevitable top terrace, and generally sound. Pegs referred to are in place except for the cave belay, but one or two extra runners may be needed.
Start at the foot of an obvious roofed groove 30ft right of King Kong.
1 120ft. 5b/c. Climb the groove to the overhang and use the fixed peg and sling to move out and up to the right. Continue straight up over a messy band and then clean, steeper rock. Move left to an obvious crack and climb it to a good stance and peg belay.
2 70ft. 5a. Climb easily to the roof, move slightly right, and go over it with two pegs for aid. Move right again and go into and up a large chimney to a good cave stance and peg belay. The pitch is rumoured to have been done free, but no confirmation is to hand.

Go Wall

3 80ft. 5a. Chimney up and move out right onto the face in a very exposed position. From a peg runner just above, either climb straight up to a gap in the vegetation, or (slightly easier—4c) go out right across a small groove and climb the short rib, passing right of the jutting overhang, into the trees. Scramble up left to the final corner chimney of King Kong.

4 30ft. 4a. As for King Kong, climb the chimney and/or the left wall to a tree belay at the top.

The Pulsating Rainbow 350ft Extremely Severe A2/3

An eliminate line giving sustained free and artificial climbing in good positions. A large and varied selection of pegs is required with a predominance of angles.

Start as for Kangaroo Wall, at the foot of an obvious roofed groove, 30ft right of King Kong.

1 100ft. 5b/c. As for Kangaroo Wall, climb the groove to the overhang and use the fixed peg and sling to move out and up to the right. Continue up over the messy band, and then leave Kangaroo by going diagonally right to a small stance and peg belays below a large patch of yellow rock underneath a black streaked overhanging wall.

2 40ft. A2. Climb straight up the indefinite groove to an etrier stance 10ft below the roof.

3 70ft. A2/3. Reach right to a long sling on a hidden peg (in place at time of writing, but if it goes, reach the peg by a tension move). Go straight over the roof into the obvious groove and peg up this for 40ft to the upper roof. Traverse 10ft right on large angles to the stance at the foot of the groove which forms pitch **4** of Technician.

4 30ft. 4c. As for Technician, climb the groove with a sling for aid, and traverse left at the top to the cave on Kangaroo Wall.

5 110ft. 5a or 4c. Pitches **3** and **4** of Kangaroo Wall.

Variants: from the upper roof on pitch **3,** instead of going right to Technician, it appears possible to go straight left to join Kangaroo Wall 20ft below the cave; however, the remaining free climbing might be too hard if hindered by rope drag or excess equipment. Someone appears to have made, or tried to make, a pitch parallel to the start of **5** by going straight up just right of the cave, presumably joining the alternative exit onto the wooded terrace.

Technician 340ft Hard Very Severe A2 ★★

A magnificent, but serious and demanding mixed climb. Ample time should be allowed as retreat and escape are problematic. Take a varied selection of pegs (none are required in quantity) and nuts are useful on pitch **2.**

Start by a large block at the foot of a thin crack 40ft right of the

roofed groove of Kangaroo Wall.
1 100ft. 4c. Climb the crack, moving right at the top round a small overhang. Step back left and continue to a belay ledge at the foot of the groove in the huge scoop.
2 40ft. A2. Mainly on nuts, climb the groove, using the crack left of the iron spike. Move slightly right at the fixed peg and continue up to an etrier stance 6ft below the roof.
3 60ft. 4c + A2. Move up and traverse right to a box shaped gap in the roof. Climb through this and continue up the wall above until it is possible to move 10ft left onto a small ledge just above the lip of the overhangs, and above the belay (some free moves). Then, using some aid, climb the wall to a belay on a ledge at the foot of a prominent groove.
4 30ft. 4c. Climb the groove using a sling for aid, and traverse left at the top to the cave on Kangaroo Wall.
5 110ft. 5a or 4c. Pitches **3** and **4** of Kangaroo Wall.

Zebrazone 160ft Hard Very Severe
This finishes on the ledge at half height and could thus be used as a bottom to Parasol or as an alternative start to Surrealist. Protection pegs need placing above the groove.
Start midway between Technician and Surrealist, in a shallow groove leaning right to a perched block.
1 120ft. 5a/b. Climb to the block and over it with care, and follow the groove which now runs straight up to a buddleia growing out of the cap. Escape left and move up left on top of a higher overhang. Make a rising traverse right for 25ft to easier ground, where the pitch could be split (peg runner or belay). From here (40ft—4c) climb straight up to a long ledge (peg and nut belays).
2 40ft. 4c. Climb diagonally right across the wall to the raised starting platform of Umbrella Girdle etc.
From here one can walk off right to the top of the scree slope.

Surrealist 320ft Mild Extremely Severe
A hard climb making considerable demands on both technique and strength. The lower wall badly needs a clean, but pitches **3** and **4** provide good and exposed climbing. Nut protection is generally good, but some pegs will be required, none of which is in place.
Start in a shallow bay at the right end of the wall, just before it curves round right and the floor rises. A groove-crack system runs up the centre of the bay with a tapering slab resting in the bottom pointing the way.
1 120ft. 5a/b. Climb over the slab and up the crack above. At its top, swing left and make a hard mantleshelf. From the left end of the ledge move up left into a corner, above which

Go Wall

traverse back right and climb a more open groove. Traverse right again to some loose blocks and climb straight up to a long ledge and peg belays.
2 30ft. 4a. Climb the corner on the right—or artificially harder its left wall—to the starting platform of Umbrella Girdle etc. (peg belay). (Escape to the right is possible from here.)
3 80ft. 5b. Traverse right along the red band to the corner at the right end of the large recess in the wall above. Enter the corner and climb it using the large flake on the right. Finish out right on a small platform on The Burning Giraffe (peg belays).
4 50ft. 5a. Move back left to an overhanging groove. Make a hard pull over the overhang and climb the crack until able to bear left to a platform below a gap in the vegetation. Move up and go left through the trees to a peg belay below the final wall.
5 40ft. 4a. Climb the wall, moving left at first and finishing out right.

Urizen 90ft Very Severe
Interesting as far as the large tree, from which one might as well abseil as continue; or the route could be linked to Kama Sutra. Start in the left of two parallel corner grooves at the right end of Go Wall where it curves round to the right.
1 90ft. 4b. Move easily up the groove to a ledge on the left wall. Continue to a small cave at the top of the groove with two hard moves facing left. Traverse left to a small tree and pull up to a slightly larger one; then move up right to a small tree and pull up to a slightly larger one; then move up right to a much larger one (50ft). Climb the loose 10ft wall to an awkward exit onto vegetation and claw a way up steep earth for 30ft with the aid of uncomfortably widely spaced trees to a belay near the top of the scree slope.

The Umbrella Girdle 370ft Extremely Severe
Useful for a wet day as the first two pitches usually stay dry, and one can then escape up or abseil down King Kong. Pitch **2** was formerly A2, and this is the first and only aid pitch at Wintour's Leap to be climbed completely clean, doubtless setting the trend for the near future. Some clusters of pegs will still be encountered; however, these should not be removed as they do duty for hanging belays and aid on Technician and The Pulsating Rainbow.
Start on the raised platform at the left end of the vegetated ledge that runs left into the wall at half height from the top of the scree slope (peg belay).
1 60ft. 4a. Descend the corner (some holds on the right make this easier than it looks), or abseil, to an obvious ledge. From

its far end climb back up a borehole to a triangular platform and peg belay.

2 100ft. 5b/c. Climb up to the roof and hand traverse left to a peg runner. Swing down on a good hold and finger traverse strenuously round a bulge to a poor resting place and good runners. Delicate moves down to the left across a slab lead to a good ledge. Move back up left to a large loose pocket (bong runner) and go horizontally across Kangaroo to various belays behind the large tree on King Kong.

3 120ft. Go easily along the ledge and pass behind a large block and a bush. Move round the edge to a small tree and go up to a larger one in the corner (belay shared with The Ragged Edge).

4 90ft. 5a. Step up and traverse horizontally left to a prominent rounded nose and climb the groove on its right. Go left again and then straight up to the two trees at the top of the long gully (Guytha).

Traverse horizontally left for 30ft on grass and rubbish ledges, and then scramble up left to the top.

Parasol 210ft Very Severe A2

An exciting line through the right end of the overhangs, taking in exposed and serious situations for the grade. Much of the aid above the roof can be done on nuts (and could probably be eliminated with determination); the peg placements are mostly good angles. Care is needed to avoid rope drag.

Start as for Umbrella Girdle, on the raised platform at the left end of the vegetated ledge which runs left into the wall at half height from the top of the scree slope (peg belay).

1 100ft. 4b + A2. Step down and traverse left into a groove (peg runner); then go left again and up to a small loose ledge (all free). Move out over the first roof on fixed pegs and up to the second. Ignoring the fixed pegs that lead out right, go slightly left until able to move out and gain the sling on the lip. Aid up the headwall in a fine position to a fixed peg. Move right and climb a groove (large nuts) to a peg runner on The Burning Giraffe. Traverse right (free) to a stance and peg belays.

2 110ft. 4a. Climb the groove behind the belay and exit onto appalling vegetation with some loose rock. Fight a way through this to the final short wall, which is climbed to the top.

It is possible (and probably preferable) to abseil from the stance at the top of pitch **1** back to the starting ledge.

It's A Beautiful Day 160ft A2/3 ★

The most continually exposed route on the cliff; it goes diagonally through the overhangs and continues traversing just above them to the chimney on Kangaroo Wall. A unique and

Go Wall

amazing line of weakness, inescapable except for a long abseil from the etrier stance. Most aid placements are good angles except for a few tied off and one rurp. Take a large selection of large angles (including 8 1"), several short blades, and a rurp or two. The first pitch is very strenuous.

Start as for Umbrella Girdle, on the raised platform at the left end of the vegetated ledge which runs left into the wall at half height from the top of the scree slope (peg belay).

1 100ft. A2/3. Climb the bulge above the platform to a ledge and make two awkward free moves left between the roofs. Continue leftwards between the roofs on pegs around a nose. Four short blades lead out to a sensational prow. Just above is a bolt. Place a rurp in a crack above, climb up to a fixed wedge, and go 10ft. left to a $2\frac{1}{2}$ bong hole. Continue left after going down one move. Not far round the edge are good pockets in a vertical crack (etrier stance; second can belay to one side).

2 60ft. A1. Follow the crack over the bulge to a good horizontal crack. Go straight left for 50ft using many large angles to the chimney on Kangaroo Wall. Small stance and peg belay down a step.

Either finish Kangaroo Wall (140ft—5a) or abseil: 150ft of doubled rope will just reach the ground.

The Burning Giraffe 380ft Hard Very Severe

Another extraordinary line of weakness, absolutely horizontal, crosses the entire wall at three-quarters height. The route follows this from the right end to the cave on Kangaroo Wall: it could possibly be extended but the section across King Kong would be very hard. Though finely situated, the climbing is unusual as the ledge is mostly too overhung to allow standing up: several sections of strenuous hand traversing alternate with shuffling on hands and knees. A few peg runners are in place, and the belay shared with Parasol is well equipped. Take plenty of large nuts.

Start as for Kama Sutra.

1 70ft. 4a. Pitch **1** of Kama Sutra.

2 70ft. 5a. Traverse easily left to the nose. Move round and continue with increasing difficulty to a small platform below a peg runner. Hand traverse on past an old wedge and swing round to a stance on the ledge at the foot of a groove (peg belays shared with Parasol).

3 130ft. 4c. Follow the fault left to the cave on Kangaroo Wall.

4 110ft. 5a or 4c. Pitches **3** and **4** of Kangaroo Wall.

Kama Sutra 180ft Hard Severe
Aptly named, the climb has some dirty bits and some interesting bits, though the two do not co-incide. The rock climbing is surprisingly easy. Urizen could be used to provide a start from the bottom of the cliff.
Start (otherwise) below the right end of the vegetated ledge that runs into the wall at half height from the top of the scree slope, at the foot of an obvious chimney groove, the rightmost on Go Wall.
1 70ft. 4a. Climb the chimney, finishing slightly left on a good ledge (peg and nut belays).
2 70ft. 4a. Climb the short wall above, and then a steep earth slope with the aid of a large tree on the left. Walk 20ft left through vegetation and then up to the final wall of Surrealist (peg belay).
3 40ft. 4a. Climb the wall, moving left at first, and finishing out right.

Variation
Direct Finish 40ft Very Severe
This eliminates the vegetation walk on pitch **2,** but is considerably harder than the rest of the climb. From the large tree at the top of the earth slope on pitch **2,** instead of going left, go straight up to a tree and block belay below an overhang.
3a 40ft. 4c. Climb the groove on the left to a fixed aid peg; then use it to move right and up to a large tree. Easy but loose ground and rubble on the right lead to the top.

Fly Wall

South of the scree slope below the path descending from the Woodcroft Quarry is Fly Wall. Straight and almost unrecessed for its 100 yard length, vertical apart from the narrow earth ledge which splits the wall from end to end at half height, its base guarded by a huge mass of tangled wild buddleia falling to the river, and only the sky above, it looks from the foot of the scree slope strangely like 'The Lost World'. The left hand half gives a number of short climbs mostly of Very Severe standard on clean, generally sound, rock. Further right the bottom of the cliff falls away and the top rises, giving longer and more serious routes which still have loose rock and vegetation. Solid layback and jamming cracks abound, and the climber is able to make full use of a wide variety of techniques. Although last to be opened up of the main walls and bays at Wintour's Leap, Fly Wall boasts more routes than any other, and there remain plenty of lines to be done.

All the climbs can be reached from either end of the wall but it is better to keep close under the rock than to scramble up from the path. The main features are described here briefly as approached from the **right** (south) end, which is best for the routes over 120ft; while in the text the start of each route is shown for an approach from the top of the scree slope, which is more convenient for the shorter climbs. The change from buddleia to forest marks the southern boundary of Fly Wall: leave the path at this point and go straight up towards the rock. The first climb, Jos'e and the Fly, is identified by an upturned block resting in a short corner. Big Fly starts half way up the rise to the left. Over this is a small dip and another short rise, at the top of which is the obvious groove of Dragonfly. Lord of the Flies starts at the foot of the next slope, Firefly a few feet to the left, and Flyover a little further left, 15ft up the next slope. At the top of this final rise is a prominent tower, Freedom, its upper part split by a diedre. Swallow's Nest is the corner on its right and Phoenix that on its left. There is a short descent to an earth platform from which rise Ecliptic and The Split. Another drop leads to Exit and Peasant, whence one can descend to a tunnel in the buddleia which leads up past the remaining climbs to the top of the scree slope. All routes finish on or near the path leading up below the quarry except Jos'e, which emerges from the woods behind the shelter. Some of the exits onto the earth and vegetation of the Main Ledge and onto the gravel and loose blocks at the top—especially on the longer, south end climbs—can be awkward, and the leader is advised to protect himself at these points, placing a peg if necessary.

Butterfly 85ft Very Severe ★
Interesting: there is a frightening looking manoeuvre on pitch
2, but several ascents have been done without mishap.
Start a few yards down the path through the buddleia from the
top of the scree slope, below a short left-facing corner.
1 45ft. Climb the corner to the ledge. Thread belay below the
crack which descends from the overhang.
2 40ft. 4c. Mount the tall block on the left. A loop is threaded
behind the overhang above (if the loop goes, place a peg in
the crack). Use a sling on the loop to gain holds on the right,
and climb the crack to the top. The only good belay is a
boulder a further 30ft back.

Moth 85ft Hard Severe
The easiest climb on the wall and short, but quite satisfying. Peg
required for main belay, or the climb could be taken in one
pitch (120ft rope is just adequate).
Start below a short wide groove, midway between Butterfly and
Peasant.
1 45ft. 4a. Climb to and up the groove (peg belay in the
corner).
2 40ft. 4b. Climb the corner to the top on good rock and holds.
The only good belay is a boulder a further 30 feet back.

Peasant 100ft Mild Very Severe
Rather dull until the final 20ft. Belay peg is not in place: it will
be a poor one anyway and, at the risk of some rope drag, it is
probably preferable to combine the pitches.
Start 25ft right of Moth below a large right-facing corner.
1 35ft. Climb the corner to a peg belay on the right below the
roof.
2 65ft. 4c. Return to the line and move up on top of the
overhang. Pass a tree and mantleshelf onto a semi-detached
flake on the right. Hand traverse right for 10ft to a ledge, from
the far right of which climb to the top on very smooth holds. A
marginally easier finish from the ledge is that of Exit on the left.
Good block belay.

Exit 85ft Hard Severe
It is questionable whether the interesting finish is worth the
struggle with earth and brambles below. Belay peg required, or
take the climb in one pitch.
Start behind a tree, just right of the large corner of Peasant.
1 35ft. 4b (in present condition). Climb up the gully moving
left onto the rib. Above, earthy slopes lead into the corner on
the right of the roof of Peasant (peg belay).
2 50ft. 4b. Climb the corner, using the right wall to start, and

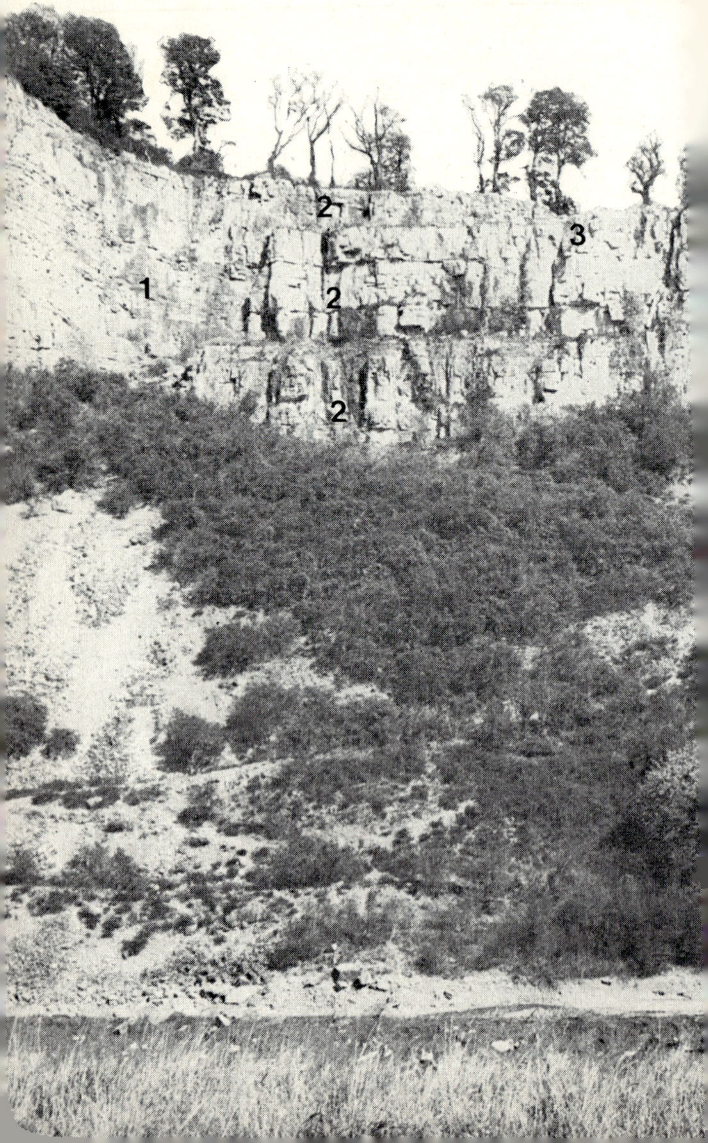
2
3
1
2
2

ly Wall
  The Woodcroft Quarry
  Moth
  The Split
  Freedom
  Swallow's Nest
  Flyover
  Dragonfly

Fly Wall

mantleshelf onto the large semi-detached flake. Climb over a shallow overhang (the Peasant hand traverse) and finish on very smooth holds (good block belay).

The Split 85ft Very Severe ★
A good climb with an uncharacteristically fine limestone layback crack. Two pegs, still in place, were used for aid on pitch **1**, but it now goes free.
Start at the left end of the grassy platform at the top of a steep earth step, reached by leaving the path below Peasant and walking 30ft right below the rock.
1 40ft. 5a. Move up to a small thread runner. Continue past two peg runners and make an awkward exit right onto the earth ledge (various nut belays under the overhang).
2 45ft. 4b. Move up under the overhang and then up to the right into the corner at the foot of the two-tiered layback crack which leads to the top (good block belay).

Ecliptic 100ft Hard Very Severe
Some bold moves on clean but potentially dangerous rock. The climb undergoes changes from time to time. The peg on pitch **2** (in place) appears to be necessary since the disappearance of a large block at foot level.
1 50ft. 4c. Climb 10ft to a grass ledge and then the corner to a larger ledge. Place a peg belay below the overhang.
2 50ft. 5a. Move up right below a smaller overhang, and over it to a peg. Use this to aid the step across the gap to the left. Climb the crack to a small unstable resting platform on the left. Continue up the crack by some strenuous and committing moves to reach easier ground and the top (good block belay).

Phoenix 80ft Hard Severe
The climb became mistakenly known as Hornix at one time. It is short but interesting and the standard is nicely maintained. There is no belay peg in place and the route could be taken in one pitch, with good nut protection.
Start below the overhung corner on the left of the tower taken by Freedom, reached by ascending a second earth step from the starting platform of The Split and Ecliptic.
1 30ft. 4b. Step up in the groove and swing out right onto the rib. Continue to a poor ledge and peg belay.
2 50ft. 4b. Move up to the right and follow the groove to the top (block belay a further 20ft back across the path).

Freedom 110ft Very Severe ★
Good climbing with the crux in a fine situation. Belay peg required; the runner on pitch **2** is in place.

Start at the foot of the prominent tower with a diedre in its middle section.
1 40ft. 4c. Climb the wall past a thread runner to a peg belay at the foot of the diedre.
2 70ft. 4c. Climb the diedre to a peg runner below the roof. Hand traverse right into the corner of Swallow's Nest and finish up this (block belay a further 20ft back across the path).

Swallow's Nest 85ft Very Severe
Worthwhile. Peg belay is in place.
Start in the obvious corner on the right of the tower taken by Freedom.
1 35ft. 4b. Climb the groove, keeping left, to the ledge and a peg belay on the left wall.
2 50ft. 4c. Take the overhang direct and continue up the groove. 10ft below the top is an awkward move onto a sloping hold. Belay a further 20ft back across the path.

Flyte 100ft Hard Very Severe
Quite a hard route. The peg runner on pitch **2** (in place) was originally used for aid, but the move goes free at the given standard.
Start 15ft right of the corner of Swallow's Nest, behind a tree.
1 40ft. 5a. Climb the wall behind the tree on small holds to a grass ledge and chockstone belay.
2 60ft. 5b. Climb up behind the belay for 20ft to a peg runner. Make a hard move up onto a small ledge high on the left, and follow the groove to the top. Block belay a further 20ft back across the path.

Flyover 155ft Hard Very Severe A1
A pleasantly varied climb. Six to eight pegs are required on pitch **2** in addition to the main belay. Take a few extra blades and small angles; a bong would be required if the wedge ceased to be functional (this has recently been renewed).
Start 15ft up left from the bottom of the long slope which descends right from Freedom and Flyte, below a small holly at 25ft.
1 85ft. 5a/b. Climb to the holly and continue slightly left to a higher bush. Move up a groove to a peg runner and make a hard traverse left into a corner, which leads to the Main Ledge (peg belays on the left).
2 70ft. 4c + A1. Climb up free to the large corner on the left. Peg up this and around the roof to the left (wedge in place) until free moves lead to the top and a good block belay.

Fly Wall

Flypast 170ft Hard Very Severe + A2
A more interesting and demanding aid pitch than that of
Flyover. Take a large selection of medium blades and angles.
Start as for Flyover.
1 85ft. 5a/b. Pitch **1** of Flyover.
2 85ft. A2. From the right end of the ledge reach and climb,
mainly on blades, an overhanging crack leading to a fixed peg
a little below a large overhanging block, which is unstable.
Move left over two overlaps and peg on up the groove to a bolt
slightly left under a long roof. Go straight over the roof and
up on good angles until a couple of awkward free moves on
loose gravel beside a pile of perched blocks lead to the top.
Block belay a further 20ft back across the path.

Firefly 190ft Hard Very Severe
Similar climbing to Flyover but a little harder. More and larger
angles are needed.
Start by a slab sitting in a short shallow groove at the bottom of
the long slope descending from Freedom. On the right is the
shorter slope leading up to the obvious groove line of
Dragonfly.
1 100ft. 5a/b. Climb the slab and groove, move out left and
up, and traverse diagonally right to a groove in the overhangs
(peg runner). Climb the groove and continue up the wall until
a short traverse right leads to three parallel short grooves. Climb
the centre one and the easy step above to the Main Ledge
below the large overhangs (peg and nut belays).
2 90ft. 5b + A2. Climb the corner (free) to the first roof and
swing round to the right to make a hard mantleshelf onto a very
small ledge. Peg up the crack to the roof and round this to the
left. The rest is free: traverse left to a long groove which leads
to the top (huge block belays).

Lord Of The Flies 180ft Mild Extremely Severe ★
An intricate route, poorly protected at first, but providing good
open climbing on the left face of the jutting prow above.
Start at a shallow brown groove at the foot of the short slope
descending left from the start of Dragonfly. This is 15ft right of
the start of Firefly and immediately below the point of the
jutting prow.
1 100ft. 5b/c. Climb the wall left of the groove and step left to
another little groove. Move left again at its top and climb
directly up to a flake crack in the band of overhangs. Swing
left into a sentry box (peg runner) and move up right into the
obvious groove which leads to the Main Ledge below the large
overhangs (peg and nut belays in the corner as for Firefly).
2 80ft. 5b. Climb the corner to the first roof and traverse 15ft

horizontally right to a small ledge below a bottomless groove
formed by an unstable looking pillar. Move up and enter this
from the right (peg runner). Exit left at the top onto another
small ledge below the final wall (peg runner) and finish up the
incipient crack slightly right into a sloping grassy bay (huge
block belays on the path above).

Dragonfly 175ft Hard Very Severe
A worthwhile route: the line is straightforward; the difficulty
well sustained. Pegs are in place.
Start at the top of the next mound right of Freedom, below a
long right-facing corner. This is the second mound from the
right of the wall, with a small dip on the right and a larger one
on the left from which rises Firefly.
1 100ft. 5a. Climb the corner past a peg runner to a good
resting ledge. Continue to an awkward exit on steep earth.
Walk left to a good thread—the peg at the foot of the crack can
then be used as a runner on both pitches.
2 75ft. 5b. Climb the steep layback crack to a small ledge, and
then the short wall on the right (peg runner). Easier but loose
ground leads to the top and a block belay on the right.

Big Fly 210ft Hard Very Severe
The longest route on the wall and serious, with some loose
rock; but worth doing for a fine third pitch. The first pitch
requires careful route-finding. All belay pegs and perhaps some
additional runners need placing.
Start half way up the right side of the first mound from the
right of the wall, below a triangular roof at 15ft.
1 90ft. 4c. Move up to the roof, or traverse in from the left; pass
to its right and reach a tree above. Bear right and then left to
ledges and a peg runner. Climb diagonally right for 25ft, past
an ivy groove, and traverse left to an exposed peg belay on top
of the overhangs.
2 40ft. 5a. Traverse left into a corner and climb up to the roof.
Make an awkward move out right and continue up to a
protruding horizontal rock spike. Fight a way through vegetation
to the Main Ledge, and belay on top of a large block at the
foot of a corner (thread and peg).
3 40ft. 5a/b. Climb the corner to a stance on the left between
overhangs (peg belays).
4 40ft. 4b. Traverse left to a dirty crack at the back of a corner
with loose sides. Climb this to the top and a good block belay.

Jos'e And The Fly 175ft Very Severe
The route improves considerably after a rather scrappy start.
Belay peg required.

Fly Wall

Start at the lowest part of the right end of the wall, by an up-turned block resting in a short corner.

1 60ft. 4c. Climb onto the block and step left to a ledge. Move up to a small overhang, right to a sapling, and then steeply left for 20ft to a tree and an airy peg belay.

2 55ft. 4c. Climb straight up for 25ft to an ivy root; then traverse left to a good thread runner. Enter the small chimney above and follow it to the Main Ledge and a tree belay.

3 60ft. 4b. A few feet left of the belay is a long flake crack, the middle section of which sounds hollow and should be treated with respect. Climb the crack to a ledge and belay on a yew tree on the right.

It is possible to climb the short wall above the yew, but the most convenient way off is to step across the wide chimney on the right and scramble up through vegetation around the bend.

First Ascent List

This is incomplete and possibly not wholly accurate owing to inconsistent documentation. It would be helpful if anyone with relevant information would write to the address given on page 11 so that the list can be improved in subsequent editions. The following are 'traditional' routes, in regular use before 1960, and published in one or other of the previous guides. There seems to be no record of the first ascents, but probably Gloucestershire Mountaineering Club parties were largely involved.

Right Hand Route, Original Route, Corner Buttress, Bottle Buttress, Central Rib I, Central Rib III, Beginner's Route

The author accepts final responsibility (though not necessarily the credit) for the form and nomenclature of the following routes, none of which has been previously published, at least in anything remotely resembling its present shape. Certainly, most or all of the pitches had been previously climbed though no records appear to exist.

The Wrong Tap (probably done in mistake for The Tap, now pitch 2 of G.N.W.R.)**, Grey Wall, Corner Buttress Routes** (arrangement thereof)**, The Problems, Cement Groove, Black Wall, Direct Route, Centre Route, Ridge By-Pass, Ridge Route, Wye Knot, Bottle Buttress Direct** (pitch 1 was climbed by D. Roberts)**, Broken Bottle, Central Rib II, This, Butterfly, Moth.**

These four routes are believed to have been done by Fred Bennett between 1966 and 1968, but no details are available of partners or exact dates; and it is not even known whether the lines described here are precisely those followed originally.

Cobra, Puma, The Ragged Edge, Kaiser Wall (first known ascent of the route described here was by E. Fivelsdal and P. Hadfield in April 1972: they found no signs of peg marks above 40ft.)

List of first known ascents: (A) alternate or varied leads

1958	June 29	**Left Hand Route**
		G.J.Frazer, J.D.C.Peacock
1958	July 13	**Great North Wall Route pitch 1** (**Symplex**)
		E.D.G.Langmuir, G.J.Frazer
1958	July 13	**Central Route**
		E.D.G.Langmuir, G.J.Frazer (A)
1961	May	**Zelda**
		J.Grieve, C.Boulton (A) (pitch 3 added on second ascent by J.Davidson)
1962	September	**The Willies**
		J.Grieve, C.Prowse
1963	April	**Prang**
		J.Grieve, C.Boulton
1963	December	**Great North Wall Route pitch 2** (**The Tap**)
		J.Grieve, C.Prowse
1963	December	**Gryke**
		J.Grieve, B.Burlton
1964	May	**Compost Wall**
		J.Grieve, D.Smith
1965	March	**Greta**
		D.T.Dove, T.Broomsgrove
1965	May	**Narcotic**
		C.F.Tanner, B.Burlton
1965	June	**King Kong**
		T.Taylor, C.F.Tanner
1965	September	**The Angel's Eye**
		T.Broomsgrove, D.T.Dove
1966	May	**Kangaroo Wall**
		F.Bennett, P.Lennard
1966	June	**Great North Wall Route pitches 3 & 4** (**Bacchanalian**)
		J.Grieve, D.Smith
1966	August	**The Early Morning Traverse**
		J.Grieve, C.F.Tanner
1966	August	**Guytha** (with alternate start)
		J.Grieve, B.Burlton
1966	August	**Technician**
		F.Bennett, P.Lennard
1966	December	**Kama Sutra**
		T.Taylor, R.Walker, J.Charlsworthy
1966	December	**Urizen**
		T.Taylor, R.Walker, J.Charlesworthy
1967	January	**That**
		T.Broomsgrove, D.T.Dove

1967	June 4	**The Burning Giraffe**
		A.C.Willmott, F.Heppenstall
1967	July 13	**The Deceiver**
		E.Fry, G.Coley
1967	August 17	**Firefly**
		Miss G.Pemberton, G.Farnsworth, C.McDonald (A)
1967	August 19	**Dragonfly**
		Miss G.Pemberton, G.Farnsworth, C.McDonald
1967	August 20	**Big Fly**
		G.Farnsworth, Miss G.Pemberton, C.McDonald
1967	September 2	**Flyover**
		G.Farnsworth, Miss G.Pemberton, C.McDonald
1967	September 10	**Flyte**
		P.Lennard, D.Target
1967	September	**Parasol**
		F.Bennett, P.Lennard
1967	October	**The Umbrella Girdle (pitch 2 at A2)**
		F.Bennett, P.Lennard
1967	October 23	**Peasant**
		D.T.Dove (top rope)
1967	December 3	**Phoenix**
		S.Eskel, M.Battle
1967	December 3	**Swallow's Nest**
		I.Ballard, G.Jarvis
1967	December	**The Split**
		P.Trinder, N.Waghorne
1967	December 12	**Freedom**
		I.Ballard, G.Jarvis, P.Henesey
1968	January	**Interstellar Overdrive**
		A.C.Willmott, J.Browne
1968	February 3	**Exit**
		P.Henessy, G.Stone
1968	June	**Surrealist**
		B.Winteringham, W.O'Connor
1968	September 22	**Ecliptic**
		M.Battle, D.King
1968	December 15	**The Pulsating Rainbow**
		A.C.Willmott, M.J.Spring (A)
1969	October 12	**Big Brother**
		F.Cannings, P.Littlejohn
1970	May	**Roger's Route**
		R.Sampford, J.Willson

First Ascent List

1972	February	**It's A Beautiful Day**
		A.C.Willmott, D.Hermelin
1973	November	**Joe's Route**
		E.Fivelsdal (roped solo)
1974	April 21	**Jos'e And The Fly**
		A.Penning, P.Creswell
1974	July 9	**Zebrazone**
		A.Strapcans, M.Putnam
1974	September 22	**John's Route**
		J.Willson, P.Curtis Hayward, A.Ashmore (part of this route had probably been previously climbed by J.Grieve and D.Smith)
1974	October 20	**Flypast**
		E.Fivelsdal, K.Lyne
1975	March 15	**The Angel's Girdle**
		J.Willson, S.Smith, N.Smith
1975	October 10	**Lord Of The Flies**
		A.Strapcans, C.King
1976	July 14	**The Umbrella Girdle** (climbed free)
		C.King, S.Gough

Index

Climb	Wall or Bay Grade	Page

Angel's Eye, The North Wall HVS ★★ — 32
Angel's Girdle, The North Wall VS ★★★ — 29

Beginner's Route, The South Bay M — 48
Big Brother North Wall XS ★ — 31
Big Fly Fly Wall HVS — 71
Black Wall Central Bay VS — 39
Bottle Buttress South Bay VD ★ — 44
Bottle Buttress Direct South Bay VS ★ — 45
Broken Bottle South Bay VS A1 — 45
Burning Giraffe, The Go Wall HVS — 62
Butterfly Fly Wall VS — 65

Cement Groove Central Bay D ★ — 39
Central Rib Route I South Bay S ★★ — 46
Central Rib Route II South Bay VS ★ — 46
Central Rib Route III South Bay VD ★★★ — 47
Central Route North Wall MVS ★ — 29
Centre Route Central Bay S (HS) — 42
Cobra Far South Bay HVS ★ — 52
Compost Wall Great Wall HS — 34
Corner Buttress Route I Central Bay VD — 37
Corner Buttress Route II Central Bay VD — 38
Corner Buttress Route III Central Bay M — 38

Deceiver, The Deceiver Buttress MXS — 49
Direct Route Central Bay D — 39
Dragonfly Fly Wall HVS — 71

Early Morning Traverse, The Far South Bay to North Wall MVS — 50
Ecliptic Fly Wall HVS — 68
Exit Fly Wall HS — 65

Firefly Fly Wall HVS A2 — 70
Flyover Fly Wall HVS A1 — 69
Flypast Fly Wall HVS A2 — 70
Flyte Fly Wall HVS — 69
Freedom Fly Wall VS ★ — 68

Great North Wall Route North Wall HVS ★ — 30
Greta Far South Bay HS ★★ — 50
Grey Wall Central Bay VS — 37
Gryke North Wall HVS — 27
Guytha Far South Bay HVS ★ — 53

Index

Interstellar Overdrive Go Wall HVS A2	56
It's A Beautiful Day Go Wall A2/3 ★	61
Joe's Route North Wall VS ★	32
John's Route Great Wall HS ★	35
Jos'e And The Fly Fly Wall VS	71
Kaiser Wall Go Wall VS A2	55
Kama Sutra Go Wall HS (VS)	63
Kangaroo Wall Go Wall XS ★★★	57
King Kong Go Wall HVS ★★★	56
Left Hand Route North Wall HS (S) ★	28
Lord Of The Flies Fly Wall MXS ★	70
Moth Fly Wall HS	65
Narcotic North Wall VS	33
Original Route Great Wall VD ★	35
Parasol Go Wall VS A2	61
Peasant Fly Wall MVS	65
Phoenix Fly Wall HS	68
Prang South Bay HVS	44
Problems, The Central Bay —	38
Pulsating Rainbow, The Go Wall XS A2/3	58
Puma Far South Bay HVS ★★	53
Ragged Edge, The Far South Bay HVS	54
Right Hand Route North Walls	31
Ridge By-Pass Central Bay M	42
Ridge Route Central Bay M	42
Roger's Route Great Wall VS	36
Split, The Fly Wall VS ★	68
Surrealist Go Wall MXS	59
Swallow's Nest Fly Wall VS	69
Technician Go Wall HVS A2 ★★	58
That South Bay S	48
This South Bay VS	47
Umbrella Girdle, The Go Wall to Far South Bay XS	60
Urizen Go Wall VS	60

Willies, The Great Wall HVS   34
Wrong Tap, The North Wall HVS   30
Wye Knot Central Bay D   43

Zebrazone Go Wall HVS   59
Zelda Far South Bay MVS ★★★   52

Appendix

A number of other routes have been recorded or reported, but for one reason or another have not been included in the body of the book. Some of them if re-established and improved could take their rightful place in a future edition, while others will doubtless lapse into permanent oblivion. Brief details are given here to prevent disappointment to would-be first ascensionists.

North Wall
Attempts have been made from time to time on the North Buttress (left of Gryke) but no records of completed routes have been forthcoming, nor is there any visible evidence. Some poor rock left of the top pitches of Left Hand Route has been climbed, but the finish is in a private garden and there is no agreed way off. Climbers are asked to regard Left Hand Route as the northern boundary of climbing on the top tier.

The Great Wall
Belvedere Route The wide grassy gully between Narcotic and Compost Wall offers a Moderate scramble, finishing in the Belvedere of the garden through which lies the way off from the North Wall: rather pointless, and discouraged by the owner, who is in all other respects favourably disposed to climbing.
The crack in the centre of the clean wall left of the top of the above route has been climbed, but is very loose.
The Left Edge takes the central section of the huge rib which divides the Great Wall in two. It is reached by traversing right from the foot of Compost Wall through brambles and nettles to a tree. The easiest way onto the rib is to climb the tree and swing down. About 60ft of climbing rather harder than the Very Difficult grade previously given leads to a cave. From here a fight with trees and ivy leads to a ledge from which it is possible to escape up Original Route to the right. (F.A. J.Grieve, C.Prowse July 1964).
Patella starts at the foot of Original Route and goes out diagonally right, presumably finishing in or around the rubbish gully left of Corner Buttress. It was not found followable from the description available, but it seems unlikely that the route is of any merit. Grade given: Severe. (F.A. D.Henry, S.Hacker, B.Heaford November 1969).

Deceiver Buttress
Torso and **Torment** appear to be two parallel short grooves on the left of the buttress, emerging after 50ft or so onto The Beginner's Route. At present they are covered by thick ivy and brambles (though a peg is visible half way up the left hand

one), but the rock seems sounder than elsewhere on the buttress and they should be worth stripping. Grades probably: 5a to 5b, Hard Very Severe. (F.A. probably F.Bennett and R.Walker 1967 or 1968).

The Trickster 15ft left of Deceiver is a long vertical crack which gives a straightforward peg pitch: avoid a hanging block at half height by transferring to the left and reach a horizontal iron spike under an overhang. 60ft A1. (F.A. E.Fivelsdal roped solo, 1973). From here it is possible to traverse (free) right to a small slab beneath an unstable overhang at the foot of an obvious groove of rotten rock. It is not known whether the groove has been climbed: an attempt by the author to lead it in 1975 ended disastrously.

20ft right of Deceiver is another A1 crack, leading to two iron crosses beneath a small overhang at 40ft. (F.A. as for pitch 1 of The Trickster). Atrocious rock in all directions barred further progress.

Go Wall

An alternative start to Kaiser Wall was made from just left of King Kong and going round in a semi-circle to the tree belay. The nature of the aid to start (a lot of bathooks in bolt holes) and of the mixed climbing higher on appalling rock precludes a rational assessment of the grade. Various people contributed to the ascent over a period. The name Metalf is written at the bottom of the cliff half way between this start and the ordinary one. This was an abortive attempt at yet another variant which ended when the enormous block fell out 20ft up.

There is a lone peg about 40ft up, 15ft right of Technician. No-one seems to know how or why it is there: a route hardly seems indicated.

Aharia is the corner groove right of Urizen. A short, fierce layback and mantleshelf is interesting (4c), but above is an 80ft catwalk on steep earth and rubbish to the top of the scree slope. (F.A. as for Urizen).

There appears to be a by-pass to the aid pitch of Parasol going directly up from the starting platform in a shallow corner.(A1?) F.Bennett noted a route **Scratch** at Very Severe somewhere on the upper half of the wall right of Parasol. This could be the arête: the rock looks very poor.

Fly Wall

Two or three unaccounted for pegs are visible indicating that other lines have been done or tried, notably a long irregular crack left of Flyover, which if cleaned could make an independent start to Flypast.

Appendix

The Woodcroft Quarry
Right of the upper half of Go Wall and set back above and behind Fly Wall is the Woodcroft Quarry. Quarrying did not finish here until 1963 and the rock is still revoltingly loose. Three or four lines have been completed but it does not seem ready yet for general use.

The Forbidden Wall
The Pool Cliff
Amphitheatre Buttress
As has been mentioned elsewhere, climbing is strictly forbidden on these three cliffs by the owners, and indeed all the woodlands south of Fly Wall, both at the tops and below right down to the river bank, is private, without any public right of access save for the Wye Valley Path described on page 18. There are also strong ecological reasons why they should remain undisturbed.

The Forbidden Wall is the large cliff immediately right of Fly Wall, and has a large terrace at two thirds height rather like the North Wall. In the early days of development a number of routes were made (mostly H.V.S.) both above and below this, notably by Hugh Banner and by Fred Bennett.

The Pool Cliff and Amphitheatre Buttree are further down river and rise directly from the bank; they can best be viewed from the other side of the river. The former, named after the superb blue pool at its foot has only one, vegetated route; though the latter, to its right, boasts four excellent hard routes, comparable with some of the best climbs in the established areas, made by Arni Strapcans and Chris King in 1975.

Thus the main lines have been done and, should the situation change, details, which are being kept and filed, could be published immediately. However, to climb or even trespass in the meantime could only prejudice relations with the locals and The Nature Reserve Management Committee, and possibly endanger the right to climb elsewhere.

The Lancaut Nature Reserve

The Lancaut Nature Reserve stretches for about 3km along the east bank of the River Wye from a point 1·5km north of Chepstow at Chapelhouse woods to the Lancaut peninsula; it extends from the river bank to the cliff top. It is managed by the Gloucestershire Trust for Nature Conservation by agreement with the land owners.

The interest in the reserve lies in its diversity of habitats—from saltings through deciduous woodlands to imposing limestone cliffs. The cliffs and woodlands provide nest sites for several interesting species of birds, and the reserve is noted for several rare and uncommon species of plants.

Public access is only along the waymarked footpath (this is the path described on page 17, and referred to there and elsewhere as the Wye Valley Path) running from Penmoel to Lancaut. There is no public access to any part of the reserve south of Penmoel.

A brochure is available giving more details of the reserve for those interested from Mrs Valerie Emmett, Prior's Loft, Tidenham Chase, Nr Chepstow.

Camping and Accommodation

Camping on the Nature Reserve is discouraged. In any case, the river banks are liable to flooding even in dry weather as the river is fully tidal here, and elsewhere the ground is very stony. Camping is possible above the village at the top of the lane to Lancaut Farm (see page 17); and permission can usually be obtained to camp at Lancaut Farm. The best site hereabouts is three miles to the north at The Beeches by Madgett's Farm (O.S. 162:552006), and this is also convenient for Shorn Cliff. A clear sign board shows where to turn left (if going north) off the B4228.

Provisions can be obtained in Woodcroft and there is a small but particularly well stocked general stores in Tutshill a few yards up the B4228 from the A48 on the right hand side; just beyond this is the doctor's surgery.

The Rising Sun Inn in Woodcroft welcomes climbers and the log book is kept behind the bar (see page 11). Food and drink are available at very reasonable prices, but not overnight accommodation. One or two farmhouses on the A48 between Lydney and Tutshill advertise Bed and Breakfast, and there is, of course, a wide range of accommodation in Chepstow.

Rescue Arrangements

Rescue equipment and a First Aid Kit provided by the Mountain Rescue Committee are kept by Mr A.P.L.James at 'Wintour's Leap',* Broadrock, Nr Chepstow.

In the event of an accident where further assistance is required, dial 999 (public phone outside The Rising Sun) and ask for the **Lydney** police, who will notify and co-ordinate the other rescue services where necessary.

After an accident, please report in writing directly to Mr H.K.Hartley, Hon. Secretary Mountain Rescue Committee, 9 Milldale Avenue, Temple Meads, Buxton, Derbyshire, giving the following details: date of accident; extent of injuries; name; age; and address of casualty; name and address of a witness; and details of MRC equipment used.

* This is the house on the bend at the north end of the long straight section of the road running along the top of the cliff. One passes through the garden on the way off from the top of the North Wall. The rescue box (which does not contain morphine) is just inside the small gate at the bottom of the garden.

Symonds Yat

Acknowledgements

Thanks are due to the following for their help, advice and encouragement in the preparation of this guide: Bob Wilson, Geoff Price and the Nottingham Climbers Club; David Langford of the Forestry Commission; Noel King and Michael Doyly of the Nature Conservancy Council; Dick Butling; Andy Houghton; Julian Pallister, Chris Milford, and The Cheltenham Mountaineering Club and especially Barry Hocken. Thanks also to all who have helped in a large number of ways and who are too numerous to mention, by checking routes and sending descriptions and other information. Finally, thanks to Susan Hope for typing the manuscript.

D.E.H.

Author's Note and General Introduction

Symonds Yat is one of those classic areas already immortalised to death in hundreds of geography texts and countless tourist guides and needs no further description. To the rock climber, however, there is one very important consideration. The area is one of Outstanding Natural Beauty and Symonds Yat itself is part of a Nature Conservancy Scheduled Site of Scientific Interest of National Botanical Importance.

The implications of this are far reaching and this section of the Wye Valley guide concerns itself with the Western Cliffs of Symonds Yat which have now been climbed on for over forty years and where little of botanical importance remains. A voluntary ban on climbing exists at the Coldwell Rocks, The Seven Sisters Rocks, and the Lord's Wood East End Crags. The three areas just named have been climbed on resulting in a large amount of damage. At present it is asked that the Coldwell Rocks be left completely alone as many rare plants, animal and bird habitats are in danger of destruction. At Lord's Wood crags there are valuable bat roosts present as well as the usual rare flora. The Seven Sisters Rocks present a different problem. Until recently climbing on the Upper Tier and the Pinnacle was without any restriction and the Lower Tier had hardly been touched because of large amounts of vegetation and loose rock. During the spring of 1975 this was removed by gardening for new routes, causing the destruction of a large number of valuable plants. The Nature Conservancy has asked that a ban on climbing be observed on all parts of the Seven Sisters until they can make an appraisal of the damage. It is possible that climbing may be allowed again by 1978 but if this request is ignored the chances will be extremely small. Again the need for these bans to be observed is stressed, remembering that a disregard for them can only damage the interests of climbers in this area, and quite possibly result in the closure of some of the crags.

D E Hope

Map

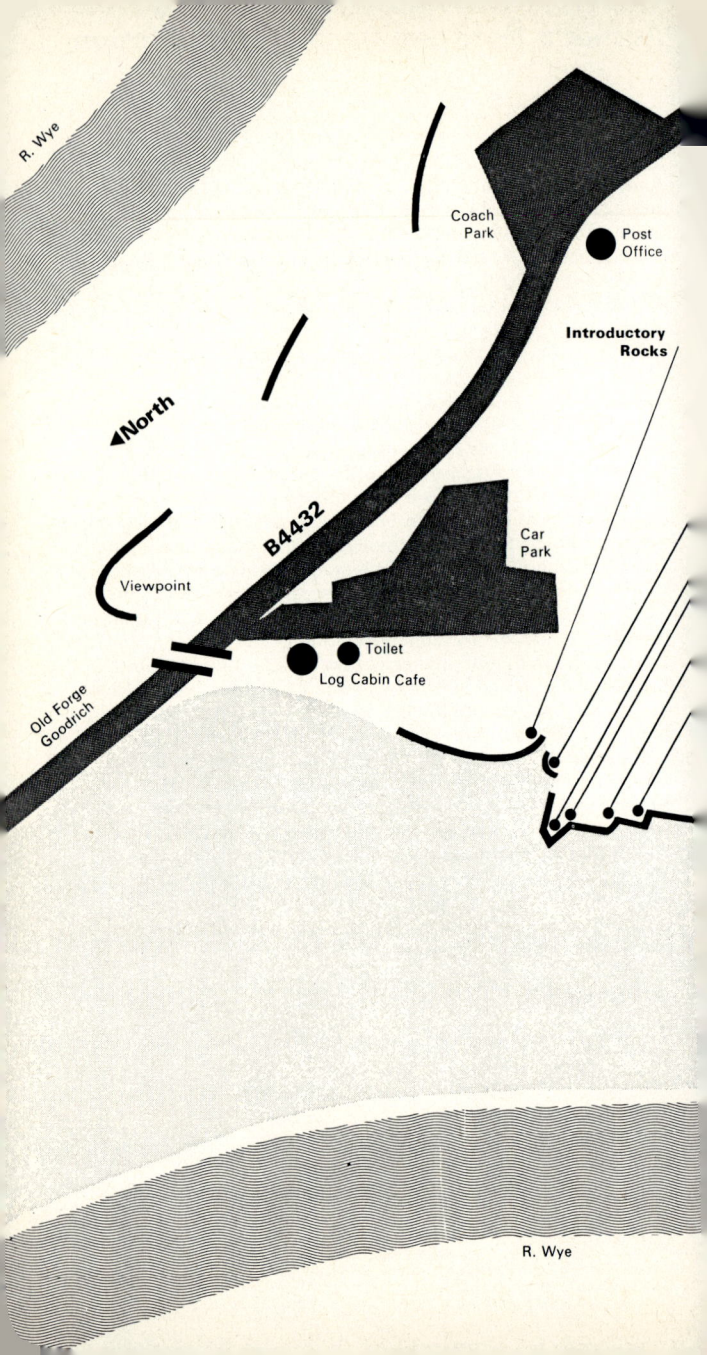

- R. Wye
- Coach Park
- Post Office
- **Introductory Rocks**
- ◀ North
- B4432
- Viewpoint
- Car Park
- Toilet
- Log Cabin Cafe
- Old Forge Goodrich
- R. Wye

stchurch
Coleford

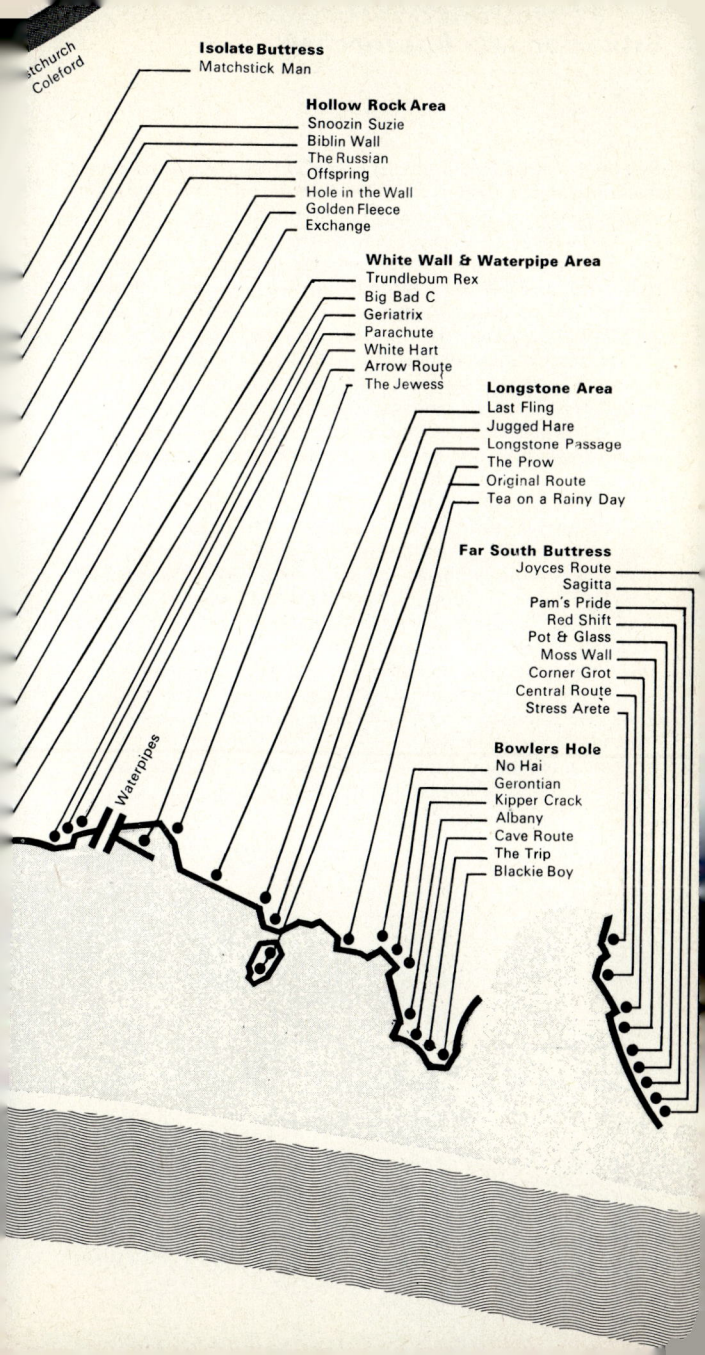

Isolate Buttress
Matchstick Man

Hollow Rock Area
Snoozin Suzie
Biblin Wall
The Russian
Offspring
Hole in the Wall
Golden Fleece
Exchange

White Wall & Waterpipe Area
Trundlebum Rex
Big Bad C
Geriatrix
Parachute
White Hart
Arrow Route
The Jewess

Longstone Area
Last Fling
Jugged Hare
Longstone Passage
The Prow
Original Route
Tea on a Rainy Day

Far South Buttress
Joyces Route
Sagitta
Pam's Pride
Red Shift
Pot & Glass
Moss Wall
Corner Grot
Central Route
Stress Arete

Bowlers Hole
No Hai
Gerontian
Kipper Crack
Albany
Cave Route
The Trip
Blackie Boy

Waterpipes

Situation and Approaches

Symonds Yat (G.R. 563157, sheet 162, 1:50,000) is situated on the Huntsham meander of the River Wye and is best approached via the A40 from Ross or Monmouth, through Goodrich or Old Forge respectively. Half way between Old Forge and Goodrich a turn south is taken over the River Wye and the narrow road is followed up the hill to reach the large car park on the top. Alternatively, from Monmouth and Gloucester, the A4136 can be taken until the B4432 is reached at Five Acres. This is followed northwards, through Christchurch, to reach the car park. The roads are signposted 'Symonds Yat Scenic Drive'. The Forestry Commission has provided a large car park for tourists and facilities include toilets and a cafe. The local people have always provided a friendly welcome for climbers and once on the crags the tourist hordes are forgotten except for the odd tin can that flies over the top. Luckily the main footpath above the crag has been fenced off because it was too dangerous and only the Bowlers Hole is now frequented by others as well as climbers. To gain access to the Western Cliffs, either go down the footpath behind the cafe which will lead to the Introductory Rocks, or walk along the forest trail path to the viewpoint at Bowlers Hole. From here a footpath leads south and then down in between the Far South Buttress and the Bowlers Hole. A footpath leads along the foot of the crags. For those wishing to stay in the area, there is a campsite at the riverside below the crags.

In case of an accident the local police are to be contacted and there is a public telephone by the coach park.

Technical

The rock is Carboniferous Limestone of the Lower Dolomite and like all Dolomitic Limestone it varies from absolutely solid to very friable and shattered. The climbs are described from left to right and are graded according to the adjectival and numerical system in general use. A numerical grade is missing where a sufficiently wide consensus of opinion was not available. Pegs for protection and aid are mentioned in the text and are usually in place. Always treat existing pegs with care (suspicion) because some have been present for a long, long time and may (will) be feeling their age. The climbs provide a wide variety of problems of surprisingly good quality, although unfortunately short. A star system is used to give visiting parties an idea of where to direct their attention if time is short. It is perhaps worth mentioning that all the climbs here have had their first chalk free ascent.

Recommended Climbs
Difficult Arrow Route
Very Difficult Snoozin Suzie ★, Trundlebum Rex, Pierre, Longstone Original Route ★
Severe Golden Fleece ★★, Joyce's Route
Hard Severe—Mild Very Severe Funky Gibbon, Offspring, Exchange ★, Big Bad C, Kipper Crack ★
Very Severe Biblin Wall, The Russian ★★★, Hole in the Wall ★, Geriatrix, The Prow ★★, Pam's Pride ★, Red Shift, Awopbopalubop Awambamboom
Hard Very Severe The Beak ★, The Ankh ★, Red Rose Speedway ★, The Trip
Extremely Severe Black Tulip ★★★

Historical

The first climb in this area is reputed to have been on one of the pinnacles at Seven Sisters, sometime in the 1930's. The first major exploration began in the late 40's and 50's, the outcome of which was the Gloucestershire Mountaineering Club's guide of 1958. In the following fifteen years various groups of climbers added their own little bits, especially those from local outdoor centres, the army, and the SAS section from Hereford. The concentration at this time was on The Seven Sisters Upper Tier and the Western Cliffs. Apart from the regular visits of these groups and some local climbers, very little happened, because the main stream of climbing was elsewhere at the time. Then the old story repeated itself—new crag X; virgin rock; miles from anywhere important, but quite accessible. So in the period between 1969-71 the Yat area was rediscovered by two groups, independently, and seemingly without knowledge of each other. The Nottingham Climbers Club made frequent visits, climbing most of the major lines on the Western Cliffs and some on the Coldwell Rocks. The second group, smaller, but a lot nearer, from Hereford (name unknown), concentrated on the gloomier Coldwell Rocks and produced a number of long and serious routes (later done by the Nottingham Climbers Club and renamed in their guide manuscript), and some shorter, pleasanter routes on the Western Cliffs.

The outcome of this activity was the production of a manuscript by the Nottingham Climbers Club, with the publication of a guide in mind. However it was decided not to publish in order to give the area a chance to breathe and to keep climbing activity at a level that would not disturb the natural habitat of the area and the wildlife within it. Unfortunately, as in many other areas, the pressures have increased and not just from climbers. The ordinary tourist now visits in vast numbers and with good facilities available the impact on the area has been immense. In the Spring of 1975 a few members of the Cheltenham Mountaineering Club decided to attempt a guide in order to minimise as much as possible the impact that an increasing number of climbers would have. Descriptions had been collected over a number of years and consequently a lot of the older routes retain their original names (as far as we know). In addition, members of the Cheltenham Club added their own quota of climbs, rediscovered others, and gave names to a few without. Once the motives behind the proposed guide were clarified, the Nottingham Climbers Club passed on their manuscript, and another small manuscript was also received from the Parkend Field Studies Centre. These were of great help in sorting out a number of problems, and the final manuscript was eventually produced.

Symonds Yat—Western Cliffs

The cliffs consist of a number of large buttresses and walls connected by short sections of broken vegetated rock and stretch for half a mile south from the slope below the Log Cabin Cafe at the car park.

There are three prominent features which aid identification of the climbing areas. From north to south these are: the Hollow Rock; the Longstone Pinnacle; and Bowlers Hole. These are marked on the general map and described in the text. There are six main climbing areas. From north to south they are

The Introductory Rocks
The Hollow Rock area
White Wall and Waterpipes area
The Longstone area
The Bowlers Hole
The Far South Buttress

The Introductory Rocks

The climbs here are short but worth recording as they provide some excellent nursery climbs. This section covers the climbs from just below the toilet block to the Isolate Buttress. Approach from the Log Cabin Cafe in the car park by going down the footpath behind the toilets for about 50 yards until the crag appears on the left. This is the north end of the Western Rocks and the climbs start almost immediately.

The first route starts at a small cave at ground level.

Garlic 20ft Difficult
Start above the right hand corner of the cave and climb the wall above it.

Gibbon 30ft Very Difficult
Starts 6ft left of the obvious sentry box. Climb to a small overhang. Swing over this moving right and follow the crack to the top.

Funky Gibbon 30ft Hard Severe
Climb into the sentry box and pull out over the block into the crack above. Follow this to the top. A fun route.

Funky Dung 30ft Very Severe
To the right of the previous climb is a steep wall with some small overhangs. Climb directly up the middle of the wall passing a small overhang at half height via a little groove in it to gain the wall above. Continue to the top trending slightly to the left.

Yew Stump Corner 35ft Very Difficult
Start at the small stump below a crack on the right and climb the crack to the top to finish below a yew tree.

Cave Wall 35ft Very Difficult
10ft to the right is a cave. Climb out of the cave at its right hand side and go up past a yew tree on the left. Care is needed with loose rock.

Chicken Run 30ft Moderately Difficult
The wide broken chimney 5ft to the right of Cave Wall. It can be climbed on its right or left hand side.

Victory V 30ft Hard Very Difficult
A good route; strenuous. Start just right of Chicken Run. Climb straight up to the obvious vee groove and go up this to the top, moving to the right, by a wider crack, to finish.

Snitch 30ft Very Severe
Five feet right is a thin crack running up the wall. Follow the crack to the top. Moving left towards Victory V by the horizontal crack is easier but cheating.

Snatch 30ft Hard Severe
Just right of Snitch are two cracks. This climb follows the left hand crack direct to the top.

Twitch 30ft Hard Severe
The right hand crack.

To the right of this is a steep blank wall with a number of problems up to Hard Very Severe in standard. These are normally top-roped and will not be described here. At the right end is a small bulge with some pockets in it. This is taken by:

The Bulger 25ft Hard Severe
The start is scratched in the rock but the first holds are easily seen. Pull over the bulge on good pockets and continue directly to the top on not so good holds.

Then follows a short wall with three tiny caves at its foot. A short climb goes up here and can be started either side of the tree.

Yew Tree Variations 20ft Difficult
Climb the wall starting on the side of the tree you prefer.

Overhanging Vee 25ft Very Difficult
This is the awkward, thrutchy vee groove, 10ft to the right of Yew Tree Variations, and has a remarkable ability to regurgitate large numbers of climbers.

10 yards to the right is Yew Tree Buttress. This has a yew tree growing at its right hand side and a small cave at its base.

Pierre 45ft Hard Very Difficult
Starts 5ft left of the cave where its name is scratched in the rock. Go up the slabby wall for 10ft to the overhang. Lean out to the right to reach good jugs, then pull over the overhang and follow the twin cracks to the top. A good climb.

Vesuvius 40ft Very Severe
Start just right of the cave and go up through the shallow groove to easier rock above which is followed direct to the top.

The Introductory Rocks

Odd-Bod 30ft Very Difficult
Takes the broken scooped wall to the right of the yew tree. Go up past the tree trending right to a ledge. Move left and finish up broken rocks.

To the right is a corner with an easy way down. This is followed by Overhanging Buttress. On its left flank is a steep, obvious crack which is wide near the bottom and closing in at about ten feet up.

Sentinel 35ft Hard Very Difficult
Follow the crack to a ledge at 20ft. Move up and right then up and left to a tree belay at the top.

Just right of the arête is a blank looking groove.

Gnome's Groan 30ft Very Severe
Start at the foot of the groove and climb it direct on small fingerholds to a good spike at 15ft. Continue directly to the top.

Just to the right is a large overhanging block below a small corner containing a small yew tree.

Goblin's Grumble 35ft Very Severe
Move up into the niche on the left of the block and then swing up into the corner and past the tree. Go up easier rocks to a tree belay. A much harder start can be had if you take the overhang on its right hand side and step left above it to reach the tree. This isn't so pleasant though.

The Isolate Buttress

To the right of Overhanging Buttress is an earthy gully—one of the easier ways down. At the top of the gully is a small buttress of rock known as the Isolate Buttress. There are two climbs.

Matchstick Man 40ft Very Severe
A fine pitch—one of the best on the crag at this grade. On the arête of the buttress is a narrow groove, getting wider as it gets higher.
1 40ft. 4c. Climb this to the wide niche at the top of the groove and then swing spectacularly right on good holds on the right arête to reach an earthy ledge and a messy scramble to tree belays.

Fat Man 30ft Hard Severe
Starts 15ft to the right and is the obvious layback crack which widens out at the top.
1 30ft. 4b. Climb the crack to gain the earthy ledge and finish as for Matchstick Man.

The Hollow Rock Area

From Overhanging Buttress the footpath runs down through a tunnel in the next major buttress. This is the Hollow Rock. From here to the White Wall is known as the Hollow Rock area. To the left of the tunnel starting on the ledge above it is:

Root Route 45ft Very Difficult
Start at the foot of a green slab with a projecting flake on its right hand side about 10ft up.
1 45ft. Climb the slab for 10ft then traverse left for 10ft until above a tree with twin trunks. Follow the leaning groove above to exit right via some tree roots.

30ft right of the tunnel, before you go through it and starting at the toe of the prominent arête which takes the skyline is:

Snoozin Suzie 140ft Very Difficult ★
Start by a large tree at the toe of the arête.
1 65ft. Go up the slab on the left of the arête to a small overhang. Pull over this to the ledge on the left and go diagonally left from this to reach a prominent crack. Climb the crack past a sapling and go up the broken wall above to a tree belay.
2 35ft. Climb up the groove behind. There is still some loose rock which needs careful handling. From the top of the groove walk along the ridge to reach a steep arête. There are two alternatives—a footpath going off to the left and
3 40ft. The arête can be climbed at the same standard to add another 40ft of climbing making this one of the longest routes on the cliff.

After passing through the tunnel, a climb can be seen making its way through the ivy covered wall to the right of the tunnel exit.

Biblin Wall 100ft Very Severe
A good climb with the crux low down and protection difficult to arrange higher up.
1 45ft. 4c. Start right of the tunnel opening and climb up over shaky holds to the overhangs. Turn these on the right by a fingery move and climb up for a further ten feet until a traverse left can be made to a stance and poor nut belays.
2 55ft. 4b. Climb the short steep wall behind the belay to a good ledge. Above the ledge is a wide groove with a tree at half height. Climb the groove keeping the tree on the right and continue to the top and tree belays. Steeper than it looks.

To the right of the Hollow Rock is a buttress which is split by a terrace. The footpath eventually reaches the right hand end of this terrace. The rock below the terrace gives poor climbing in contrast to the impressive overhanging upper part. The first two climbs start some 40ft to the right of the Hollow Rock.

High Jack 100ft Hard Very Severe
1 40ft. Climb the shattered groove to reach the terrace. Belay under the prominent overhanging crack of The Navvy.
2 60ft. Walk 10ft left until you are under the recessed overhang at the left hand end of the terrace. Climb up to the overhang and move awkwardly right to discover not a little exposure. Gain the crack above and climb this in good situations to reach the top and tree belays.

The Navvy 90ft Hard Very Severe
1 40ft. Climb the shattered groove as for High Jack to reach the terrace.
2 50ft. 5a. A brutish looking crack punches its way through the overhang above. Strenuously pick your way through this to reach the top and tree belays.

Phizzog 90ft Very Severe
Starts 50ft right of Biblin Wall and about 10ft right of the previous route, near a multi-trunked tree by the side of the path.
1 90ft. 4c. Climb the broken wall for 20ft to a short vee groove in the overhang and pull through this to the terrace. Above is an intimidating looking overhang with some black streaks on the rock. Climb the thin crack on the right to reach the overhang, then using good jugs on the lip, swing left into the groove and go up this to the tree. Step left onto the steep wall and go diagonally left for 25ft to reach a good ledge and tree belays.

Diamond Groove 110ft Very Severe
Starts 5ft right of the previous route and directly opposite the multi-trunked tree, at a groove with a small brown scar on its right hand side.
1 80ft. 4b. Go up the groove to the terrace, to arrive just below an overhanging groove. Go up into the groove until it closes in an inverted vee. From here swing spectacularly left into the next groove and go up this and the wall above, trending right to a tree belay.
2 30ft. Go easily up the arête behind the tree to the top.
2a Right hand variation. 50ft. 4b. From where the overhanging groove closes in an overhanging vee, go diagonally right for 10ft to reach a crack. Follow this to the top and tree belays.
2b Direct variation. 35ft. 5a. From where the overhanging groove closes in the overhanging vee go up straight to the top.

The Hollow Rock Area

The Beak 85ft Hard Very Severe ★
This route is surprisingly good although it takes an unimpressive line. As one gets higher, the blocks providing good holds jut out further and further thus providing an element of strenuousness which combines well with their looseness to provide one of the more serious routes of this grade on the cliff. The climb starts at the right hand end of the terrace below a broken crack and just to the left of the corner of The Russian.
1 85ft. 5a. Climb the easy rock to the broken crack and follow this until it closes at a jutting loose block. Pull straight over this and move slightly left to reach a thin crack and an old peg runner. Make an awkward move past the peg using another loose block until the steepness wears off. Continue up the crack for a further 10ft until a step right around the rib is made and finish up a little shattered wall as for Scooby Doo.

Scooby Doo 80ft Hard Very Severe
The route climbs the arête of the left wall of The Russian.
1 80ft. 4c. Start below the broken crack just a few feet left of the arête. Climb the easy rock to gain the crack. Follow the crack on large holds until a short bulge is reached. Step right into a small corner which leads into the short groove above. Go up this and finally step left onto the arête and climb easily up a little shattered wall to a ledge and tree belay. The quality of the rock is much better than it appears at first sight.

The Russian 100ft Very Severe ★★★
This is the obvious corner just to the right and is one of the main features of this part of the cliff. A fine route.
1 70ft. 4c. Climb the wall to the bottom of the corner. Some trying moves lead to an old ring peg. Continue up the corner to turn the final steep section on the right.
2 30ft. As for Diamond Groove or walk off.

Mockingbird 100ft Very Severe
A good climb. Starts 20ft right of The Russian at the same place as Red Rose Speedway. The climb takes the groove to the left of Red Rose Speedway.
1 80ft. 4c. Climb to the ledge at 10ft as for Red Rose Speedway and walk left to the groove. Climb this for 40ft to a ledge just below a bulging wall with some large pockets in it. Step left to a grassy ledge and go up the steep wall above to another ledge and tree belays.
2 20ft. Climb the broken groove behind to the top.
(Note: The original climb on this line was Newcastle Arms but instead of taking the groove direct it went up the vegetated ledges to the left of the groove and joined up again for the final

wall. Mockingbird is included as the pleasanter of the two alternatives.)

Red Rose Speedway 100ft Hard Very Severe ★
Takes the steep leftward slanting crack in the red wall 20ft right of The Russian and 20ft left of Otfspring. The crack is very sustained.
1 100ft. 4c. Climb up 10ft to the ledge at the start of the crack. Continue to where the wall bulges. Some awkward moves over this lead to a good hold. Go straight up the crack above until it is possible to step right to a small tree. Continue directly to the top.

Lord of the Dance 90ft Very Severe
5ft to the left of Offspring a broken rounded rib leads to a small overhang guarding the entrance to a groove in the wall above.
1 90ft. 4c. Climb with difficulty to the overhang and pull over this to gain the groove above. Climb this for 20ft when it ends and traverse left for 10ft until a broken groove is reached. Follow this to reach the large ledge at the top of Offspring. Finish as for Offspring via the easy groove.

Offspring 90ft Mild Very Severe
The twin cracks in the corner to the right of Red Rose Speedway make this route one of the obvious features of the cliff. A good route.
1 65ft. 4b. Climb the cracks throughout until a grassy bay is reached.
1 25ft. Finish up the back right hand corner of the grassy bay.

The Wasteland 80ft Extremely Severe
An improbable line taking the blank wall between Offspring and The Ankh. Start 5ft right of Offspring.
1 80ft. 5c. Climb the wall for 15ft, then make a hard move over the bulge to reach a small ledge. Climb straight up for 10ft to reach the overhang and climb this to gain the narrow groove above and some good pockets. Climb straight up from the narrow groove to the top and tree belays.

The Ankh 80ft Hard Very Severe ★
Starts 15ft right of Offspring by a leaning block at the foot of the crag. Originally climbed with a peg for aid, subsequent gardening revealed another hold and the peg was dispensed with.
1 80ft. 5a. Climb up the vague crack line and over a small overhang to reach a resting place. Continue up the same direct line until the large overhang is reached (poor protection peg).

The Hollow Rock Area

From here traverse 10ft left to the narrow groove of The Wasteland and follow this to the top.

Black Tulip 100ft Extremely Severe ★★★
Two very fine pitches make this one of the best routes on the cliff. Originally climbed with a bolt for aid, then for protection only, and finally eliminated altogether.
1 50ft. 5c. Start below the impending wall below the 'Hole in the Wall' cave and just to the right of the leaning block at the start of The Ankh. Climb the wall to a good jug on the lip of the overhang. Manipulate until your feet are on the jug and then move up the wall to a thin crack with a hold on a shaky flake. Ten feet higher and to the left is a thread runner. From this move up towards the overhang and avoid it by climbing diagonally right to reach the cave and a massive thread belay.
2 50ft. 4c. Move right from the cave and climb the overhanging groove. At the top of the groove move right with difficulty onto a small ledge and climb the overhanging wall above on good holds.

Hole in the Wall 100ft Very Severe ★
15ft to the right of Black Tulip is a corner. This good route starts up it.
1 55ft. 4b. Climb the corner with increasing difficulty until a move right leads to a ledge. Go straight up for 10ft then traverse left into the cave and a thread belay to end all thread belays.
2 45ft. 4c. From the left hand opening of the cave make a difficult move up the groove behind the cave to reach good holds. Follow these to the top and plentiful tree belays.

Peacock 100ft Mild Very Severe
The shallow groove to the right of Hole in the Wall, marks the start.
1 100ft. 4b. Climb the groove and crack to where it disappears and swing right onto the earthy ledge. From here go up a wall for 10ft and then move diagonally left and up into a groove which is followed to the top.

Yorker 90ft Hard Very Severe
Only 60ft of climbing on rock. Starts between the groove of Peacock and the ramp of Grobbler, and takes an indefinite crack leading to a short white groove some 30ft above the ground.
1 90ft. 4b. Climb directly up to the groove. Climb this and go up the steep wall above it on good pockets to reach a depressingly dirty scramble to finish. Protection is very poor.

Grobbler 80ft Mild Very Severe
The wall to the left of Golden Fleece contains a steep ramp. Start directly below this.
1 80ft. 4b. Climb up to the base of the ramp and continue up this until it merges into the corner of Golden Fleece. Finish up this.

Golden Fleece 80ft Severe ★★
The large clean cut corner on the right hand side of this first main bay of rock is the most prominent feature on this part of the cliff and it provides an excellent climb.
1 80ft. 4a. Climb the corner. Just below the top a step left has to be made to reach good holds and a tree.

The Druid 90ft Very Severe
Another good climb, on the steep right wall of Golden Fleece. Start 5ft right of Golden Fleece below some thin cracks.
1 90ft. 4b. Follow the cracks for 40ft until they fade away and then step left to reach some big pockets below the overhang. Turn the overhang on its right hand side and step left above it onto the ledge on top of the overhang. Climb up for a few feet then go diagonally right to reach a break on the arête and continue up the earthy groove behind to reach the top and tree belays.

15ft to the right of Golden Fleece, the arête contains a groove.

Exchange 80ft Mild Very Severe ★
A good open climb.
1 80ft. 4b. Climb the groove for 20ft until a step left is necessary to follow the kink in the groove. Continue directly to the top of the groove and scramble to the top and tree belays.

Beyond this is a broken section of crag with some rather scruffy routes which are not described. Some 20 yards right a prominent cracked groove is met.

Flying Machine 40ft Very Difficult
1 40ft. Climb the groove/crack to the large tree at the top and then make an ornithological move left to reach the large tree branch about 5ft away. Swarm up this to an earthy ledge. Descend by the easy chimney on the left.

30ft right is a large block in the path. Above this are two cracks running up the wall.

The Hollow Rock Area

Green Grow The Grollies Oh! 70ft Very Severe
1 70ft. 4b. Climb up to where the crack on the right passes through a bulge. Pull over this to a ledge and continue up to where the crack widens and gets steeper, just below some small overhangs on the left. Traverse 10ft left below the overhangs to reach a white groove and go up this to the top. Care is needed with loose rock in the upper part of the route which has a habit of providing an excess of adrenalin in many climbers.

Another 20ft right is a small semicircular bay. On the left hand side is a steep crack and on the right is a bottomless chimney with a small cave 15ft up on the left of the chimney.

Trundlebum Rex 80ft Very Difficult
The crack on the left of the bay.
1 40ft. Climb the crack, steep and awkward at first, to a good ledge and tree belay.
2 40ft. Scramble up to the right for 10ft to another ledge just to the left of a shallow cave. Climb the short groove on the left of the cave for 10ft then step right into the groove above the cave. Climb this to broken rocks and go over these to the top. The alternative to this pitch is a messy 60ft scramble to the left.

Big Bad C 80ft Hard Severe
A good route with an entertaining start.
1 80ft. 4b. Step up into the niche at the bottom of the chimney and surmount the overhang to get to the upper part of the chimney. Follow this for 30ft until a step left to a ledge can be made. Continue up two short grooves to a slightly loose finish. A variation start can be made by climbing up the steep wall to the left of the chimney in order to reach the cave direct, from where the chimney can be regained easily.

The White Wall

From this small bay (described above) the path continues past a wall covered in ivy to reach a large, white wall. 10ft right of the ivy curtain is a prominent groove, 20ft up on the face.

Strathdon 90ft Hard Very Severe
Start directly below the groove.
1 90ft. 5a. Climb the steep wall to the bottom of the groove. Proceed delicately to the top of the groove and up the steep wall above until a prominent traverse line left can be taken to a good ledge. A belay could be taken here if so wished. Finish up the short groove behind.

The Bell 80ft Hard Very Severe
The overhang on pitch 2 makes this an exciting route. Start by a tree at the middle of the wall, 20ft right of Strathdon.
1 60ft. 5a. Climb straight up the wall on dubious holds for 10ft. Traverse left on undercuts (loose) to a good resting place in a scoop. Climb the groove above for a few feet and then trend diagonally right across the overhanging wall to reach easier ground and the cave. Poor belays.
2 20ft. 4c. From the left hand side of the cave climb powerfully over the roof to reach big jugs. Amble off right to the top.

Yates 90ft Very Severe
Start at the tree at the beginning of The Bell.
1 90ft. 4c. Climb up the slab on the right to reach the big overhang. Traverse left underneath it to reach the groove on its left hand side. Follow this groove to a cave and continue on up the final small groove above to reach tree belays. Protection is poor on the lower section of the climb.

Britannia 80ft Hard Severe
Starts as for Yates.
1 55ft. 4a. Go diagonally right across the slab for 20ft until a shaky block is reached. From the block step awkwardly right into the bottomless groove and go easily up this to some large ledges and a cave.
2 25ft. 4b. Step left out of the cave and go up the white groove above to the top. A nice pitch.

Priory 90ft Very Severe
Starts just left of the arête which marks the right hand end of White Wall.
1 90ft. 4b. Go up the shattered wall to the left of the old ivy root. At the bottom of the obvious ivy filled crack is a good thread runner. From here step left into the groove running up the centre of the wall and climb up this to the top of it where a

The White Wall

step left around its left wall can be made to reach good ledges and belays. Scramble to the top.

Geriatrix 90ft Very Severe
A fine climb with some excellent loose rock. Starts to the right of Priory by the foot of the arête.
1 90ft. 4c. Climb the arête by whatever means seem appropriate and at 25ft go into a short groove on the left and up this to a ledge and the thread on Priory. From here make some hard moves for 10ft on the arête and move right into the big bottomless groove and climb on up the continuation crack from the groove, which runs up the steep wall above, to the top.

The Waterpipe Bay

20ft right of the arête is a large tree at the left hand end of the Waterpipe Bay.

Parachute 90ft Severe
1 40ft. Climb the tree for 15ft until it is possible to step into a wide crack. Follow this for 10ft and then go up twin cracks until a step right to a terrace and tree belay can be made.
2 50ft. Climb the pleasant groove behind to the top.

The Fox variation. Harder than the groove.
2a 45ft. Step left and climb the wide crack to the top of the pinnacle. Scramble from here to the top.

White Hart 90ft Hard Very Severe
Starts 10ft to the right of the tree by a small slab with a thin crack on its left hand side and an overhanging flake at 10ft.
1 40ft. 4b. Climb up the slab to the overhang and layback round this to reach the crack above it which leads to the terrace and tree belays.
2 50ft. 5a. 5ft right along the terrace is a magnificent leftward eaning groove. Climb over the bulges to reach the foot of this and follow it to the top. Climb the short wall above with some difficulty. The climber expecting excellent protection will be a little disappointed.

20ft right of White Hart and 15ft left of the waterpipes is a short steep groove.

Slidewater Shuffle 90ft Severe
1 40ft. 4a. Climb the groove to reach the small ledge on the right hand side at the top of the groove. Continue directly up the steep wall to the terrace and a tree belay.
2 50ft. 4a. Behind the tree is a steep wall and above this an obvious groove. Climb the wall to the groove and up this to the top taking care with the tottering pinnacle flake that constitutes the last few feet. Also beware of some rotten tree roots which could precipitate rapid downward movement if treated with disrespect.

Right of the waterpipes there is a section of broken rock some thirty yards long, until a small, compact piece of rock is met. There is an obvious triangular pulpit of rock about 30ft up. The right hand side of this is a groove which is taken by the next climb.

Arrow Root 80ft Difficult
1 50ft. Pull over the initial overhang and follow the groove to

The Waterpipe Bay

its top and a tree belay.
2 30ft. Go up the broken easy rib behind the tree, or walk along the ledge to the right where a number of different finishes can be made.

The first groove along this ledge is:

Rootin Toot 25ft Very Difficult
1 25ft. Climb the groove passing a tree at 8ft. Some loose rock.

Broken Root 30ft Moderately Difficult
1 30ft. 10ft right of the previous climb is a broken gully. Climb this.

Otak 30ft Hard Severe
Start 15ft right of Broken Root. Begin from a block at the foot of a leaning wall.
1 30ft. 4b. Climb diagonally right for 10ft to a good jug and pull over the overhang on this until a crack behind a block is reached and you can stand in balance. Climb straight up from here to the tree above. An exciting little climb.

Rite Root 20ft Difficult
Starts 20ft right of Broken Root. Climb the short groove in between two old ivy roots, passing a large tree and continue up the broken slab to the top.

From the start of Arrow Root the footpath runs below a further thirty yards of scruffy rock until a number of caves are met. A steep earthy path branches off here to the left and leads to a steep section of rock with a cave in the corner. This path leads off left along the ledge previously mentioned and the four routes just described can be reached without doing the first pitch of Arrow Root if so wished. To the right of the cave there are three routes.

The Jewess 40ft Extremely Severe
A serious fingery route with no protection. The first ascent was soloed after a top roped ascent.
1 40ft. 5b. Start at a block to the right of the cave below a leaning wall with some small pockets in the lower section. Climb the steep wall above the block on pockets trending slightly to the left. At 15ft up move diagonally right across the wall to reach the top of the right hand arête and good holds. An exciting climb.

Big Girl 50ft Hard Very Severe
1 50ft. 5a. Start as for Dave's Downfall. Climb up to the overhang and traverse left into the groove. Become instantly slimmer and climb through this (strenuous) and continue to the top over some loose blocks to reach a yew tree. A harder direct start can be made to reach the overhang.

Dave's Downfall 50ft Hard Severe
Starts 10ft left of the cave by the footpath.
1 50ft. 4b. Climb the wall on good holds just to the right of the overhang. Step right into a scoop and go up this for a few feet passing a yew tree until a step left can be made onto a broken wall. Go up this trending slightly left to reach the big yew tree at the top.

Drunk 60ft Very Severe
Start from the top of a small pedestal of rock at the left hand side of a cave about ten feet right of the start of Dave's Downfall.
1 60ft. 4c. From the pedestal move up trending slightly right for 12ft then make a difficult move up and left and continue until a small groove is reached. Finish up this to reach tree belays.

Loony on the Loose 65ft Mild Very Severe
Starts at the right hand side of the cave.
1 65ft. 4b. Go up the rib on the right hand side of the cave to reach a small tree. From here go diagonally up and left to reach the right hand of two grooves. Climb this to exit on an earthy series of ledges. Quite a good climb except for its messy finish.

The Longstone Area

The caves on the main footpath mark the start of the Longstone area.
The small caves are marked with painted numbers.

Nikabrik 65ft Difficult
Start just to the right of C11.
1 65ft. Climb a steep wall to reach a ledge. Climb diagonally right and up the slabby rocks to a messy finish.

Last Fling 70ft Hard Very Difficult
Start from the left hand end of the first large cave to the right of Nikabrik.
1 70ft. Traverse left for 10ft from the left hand side of the cave to a comfortable standing position. Go up from here to reach a ledge. Step right and go up diagonally to the right until the final steep wall is gained. Just to the right of a dead yew tree is a narrow earthy groove in the wall. Climb this and finish up the small leaning groove above to reach a tree belay.

Beyond the large cave are two more caves.

Porridge 30ft Very Difficult
Start at a large tree to the left of these two caves.
1 30ft. Step onto the wall by the tree and go diagonally right up the groove. Climb this for 5ft, then go up the right wall and finally step back left to finish up broken rocks.

In between the two caves is a rib with a small overhang 5ft off the ground.

Lurcher 30ft Mild Very Severe
1 30ft. 4b. Pull round the overhang to the left. Step back right and go directly up the strenuous broken groove to the left of a prominent yellow patch of rock, in order to gain easier angled rock and the top.

Jugged Hare 30ft Difficult
1 30ft. 5ft right of the second cave is a little leaning wall, covered in holds. It can be climbed almost anywhere at the same standard.

20ft right is a broken gully in a nose of rock, directly opposite the Longstone Pinnacle. This gully is known as the Longstone Passage and gives a climb of moderate standard, doubling as an easy way down. There are a number of climbs on the Longstone. We only describe the two best, leaving the others to be found by you. The most obvious is a girdle traverse of severe standard.

The Original Route 50ft Very Difficult ★
Starts from the shoulder which joins the Longstone to the main face and opposite the easy way down.
1 50ft. From the shoulder pull up over the jutting prow to a ledge. Climb up to reach a scooped wall with a metal spike in it. Climb directly to the top from the spike.

A large block belay is convenient for abseiling off, but more than one party has had to reclimb the route to free a jammed rope.

The Prow 130ft Very Severe ★★
A fine climb in one of the best situations in the area. Start at the foot of a small groove at the foot of the arête on the river face.
1 70ft. Climb the groove for 20ft then step left into the next groove. Follow this passing two old protection pegs to reach a ledge on the left and poor peg belays in place.
2 60ft. Step left from the belay and pull up on a large and very shaky block to two old rusty protection pegs. Traverse left for 5ft to the bottom of the final crack. Climb this to the top and a superb view. Descend via the Original Route or by abseil.
2a Orange Wall variation 55ft Very Severe
Leave the belay and make for the two rusty old protection pegs above and to the left. From here traverse right beneath an overhanging arête for about 10ft and move up to a small ledge at the base of a wall covered in orange lichen. Traverse left along the ledge and make a bold move to gain the left edge of the wall and a strong pull up on good pockets. The route then goes straight up to the top and belay. Now rather loose.

Back on the main cliff and 30ft right of the easy way down is a rightward slanting green slab with some grey patches of rock at the bottom left hand side.

Staircase 35ft Very Difficult
1 35ft. Climb the slab for 20ft, trending diagonally right until good holds and easier rock enable a direct line to be taken to the top.

10ft right at a horizontal slot just off the ground is a steep scoop leading to a large pocket, 15ft up at the top of the scoop.

Bannister 30ft Very Difficult
1 30ft. Climb the scoop to reach the pocket. Step left to easier angled rock and go straight up to the top.

The Longstone Area

Arch Wall 30ft Very Severe
1 30ft. 4b. Climb straight up from the right hand end of the horizontal slot to an old ivy root and continue to a small overhang which is climbed by a beak of rock on its right hand side. Continue up the wall above to the top.

On the right hand side of the cave is an easy angled groove.

Tea on a Rainy Day 45ft Hard Difficult
1 45ft. Climb the groove throughout to the top. A pleasant climb.

The Bowlers Hole

From the last climb another broken and vegetated section is passed for approximately thirty yards, until a small rectangular bay of rock is reached just before the footpath drops steeply down to the bottom of the large buttress on the right. This buttress is Bowlers Hole, a famous beauty spot and viewpoint. The rectangular bay is the northern flank of Bowlers Hole and provides a lot of short but enjoyable climbs which we feel are worth recording. On the left hand side is a groove with a mossy wall and rib to its left. Routes have been done here but are not worthwhile.

To the right are some huge fallen blocks which lie at the left hand corner of the bay.

No Hai 30ft Very Difficult
1 30ft. The left hand corner is climbed by stepping from the blocks onto the wall at the foot of the corner and going straight up to the top without deviation to the crack a few feet to the right.

Bookworm 30ft Severe
1 30ft. Pull strenuously into the crack and follow it to the top to exit a few feet from the top by stepping right to a slab and some tree roots.

Bludgeon 30ft Very Severe
1 30ft. 4c. Immediately right is a leaning wall with an overhang at the bottom and an overhang at the top. Turn the first overhang by a short groove on its right then step left to the ledge above it and climb the wall and top overhang direct to reach the top.

Claptrap 30ft Very Severe
1 30ft. 4b. Start as for Bludgeon, up the short groove to reach the blind crack immediately right of Bludgeon. Follow this crack to the top.

Gerontian 30ft Very Difficult
1 30ft. The prominent crack splitting the centre of the bay. Enter the crack from the left wall and climb it to the top.

Mango Highway 30ft Very Severe
The red wall to the right of Gerontian has two trees at its foot. Directly above the trees is a thin steep rightwards leaning ramp.
1 30ft. 4c. Climb directly up the wall from the trees, using some small pockets to reach the ramp. Continue up this then up the wall above to the top.

The Bowlers Hole

Kipper Crack 35ft Hard Severe
1 35ft. 4b. The prominent crack on the right hand side of the bay is one of Symonds Yat's famous test pieces. Climb the crack unless you understand what famous test pieces are all about.

Kebbo 40ft Severe
Start at the right hand side of the wall, 20ft right of Kipper Crack.
1 40ft. 4a. Swing right around the arête into the slim groove on the arête and follow this to the top, keeping to the arête. A nice climb with some good positions.

From the right hand side of this rectangular bay, a narrow terrace leads from the foot of Kebbo across the main buttress of Bowlers Hole, at half height. This reaches its end at a large cave in the centre of the buttress. The following two routes cross this terrace and start at the foot of the buttress. The path leads steeply down a muddy slope to a small bay of rock below the large cave. The left hand side of the bay is marked by a blunt mossy rib. Just to the left of the rib is a yew tree.

Albany 110ft Severe
Starts in a mossy groove to the right of the tree.
1 45ft. 4a. Go up the groove trending slightly right for about 30ft. Step right onto the arête and go up to the terrace and a tree belay.
2 65ft. 4a. Walk 10ft right and pull over a bulge into the bottom of a red groove and climb up to the small tree on the left. Traverse 15ft left on good holds to just below a big yew tree. Climb directly to the tree to finish.

Salutation 110ft Hard Severe
5ft to the right of the rib is a groove leading up to the terrace.
1 45ft. 4b. Climb the groove to the terrace and a tree belay.
2 65ft. 4b. From the left hand side of the cave a steep wall leads into an obvious groove. Climb into the groove and follow it to the top.

In the middle of the bay are two small caves. Immediately left of the bottom cave, is a broken crack which leads into the impressive left hand groove in the upper buttress. This gives:

Cave Route 100ft Hard Very Severe
1 50ft. Follow the broken crack via the two small caves to reach easy rock leading into the big cave for a rest.
2 50ft. 5a. Leave the cave on the right and climb the groove

past a protection peg and follow on to the top.

The Trip 100ft Hard Very Severe
15ft right is a messy crack.
1 100ft. 5a. Climb up this to where it opens out into the wall above. Climb across the wall moving diagonally left to some threads and a small cave. From here move diagonally right to reach an aid peg in the yellow wall. From the peg enter the groove above and go up this to the top.

15ft right and just 5ft left of a large yew tree is a short corner 10ft up above an earthy ledge.

Blackie Boy 100ft Severe
1 65ft. 4a. Climb carefully over the earthy ledge and up the corner to gain the large vee groove above. Climb this and continue over easy vegetated rock to a belay behind a large pulpit block.
2 35ft. Climb directly up the wall behind and finish up a scoop. This brings you out at the Bowlers Hole viewpoint.

Awopbopalubop Awambamboom 230ft Very Severe
Although artificial in line and easily escapable practically anywhere on the route, this climb offers some good situations as it wanders its way across the upper part of the Bowlers Hole on huge jugs.
1 65ft. 4a. As for Blackie Boy.
2 30ft. 4b. On the left wall behind the pulpit there is a ledge fading away towards the arête. Go across this until a step left around the arête can be made to reach an airy stance and a belay. Please do not disturb the occasional nesting pigeon.
3 55ft. 4b. From the stance go up and to the left for a few feet until a step left can be made to reach the upper crack of The Trip. Continue left until the groove of Cave Route is reached and make an awkward move left around its left arête. This brings you onto the lip of the cave roof. An obvious line of footholds along the lip leads to a tree and a belay from which you can savour the position.
4 20ft. 4b/c. From the tree climb down diagonally to the left across a steep wall to reach a good ledge in a groove. Climb down the groove for a few feet and belay on a ledge with an old tree stump. This is necessary because the second could not be protected adequately from the final belay. A backrope around the previous belay tree is recommended.
5 60ft. 4b. Climb back up the groove to reach the good ledge. From here step up and move left around the arête. Continue moving left and slightly downwards until two saplings are

The Bowlers Hole

reached, one at foot level and the other at head level. Traverse a further 20ft left to reach a groove with a bundle of saplings at its base. Step left around the arête and go 20ft diagonally left and up across vegetated slabs to reach the top and tree belays.

The Far South Buttress

Best reached by using the footpath along the top of the crags to reach the Bowlers Hole Lookout. From here a smaller path runs south until a right fork can be taken down a muddy path. The rocks can be seen on the left side of the main path, which leads down to the river, and a few yards down this another path leads off left to the buttress. The first climb takes the easy angled wall just past the first messy vegetated section and to the right of a large tree.

Travellers Rest 70ft Difficult
Start below and to the right of the tree.
1 70ft. Climb an obvious line to the trees and to a large ledge behind. Climb directly up from here, passing a tree at mid height.

Stress Arete 60ft Hard Very Severe
Takes the arête to the right of a short wall where the path meets the cliff. Start up a small groove leading to a cave and a large earthy ledge.
1 60ft. 5a. Climb the groove to a big ledge and the cave. Step right onto the blunt arête and climb this past a peg (protection) to the small triangular nose at the top. Pass this on its right and finish up a short wall and crack.

40ft right is another arête, just right of a small cave.

Central Route 65ft Very Difficult
1 65ft. Follow the blunt arête until it becomes sharper at half height. Keeping just left of the arête, go directly up to a big yellow patch of rock and finish up this.

Immediately right are two large caves in a small bay guarded by two trees.

Mellow Yellow 45ft Hard Very Severe
At the left hand side of the left hand cave is a thin crack running up a yellow groove.
1 45ft. 5a. Climb the steep wall on the left of the cave for 5ft to reach the crack and then follow this to the top. Sustained.

At the right hand side of the right hand cave is a yellow groove 10ft up.

Yellow Peril 40ft Hard Severe
1 40ft. 4a. Climb the short wall on the right of the cave to reach the groove. Go up this for 10ft until a step left can be made to a good foothold. Climb the yellow rock above for a few

The Far South Buttress

feet then move right back into the groove and finish directly over the small overhang above.

To the right of Yellow Peril is a mossy slab with a broken corner on its right.

Julep 30ft Hard Very Difficult
1 30ft. From the foot of the corner, climb diagonally left until the centre of the slab is reached and then continue directly to the top.

Cornergrot 30ft Difficult
1 30ft. Climb the broken corner to finish by a tree—a scruffy climb.

To the right of this bay is a large red wall with several small caves in it. The cave on the left is the largest and below its right hand side is a stairway of easy rock.

Moss Wall 70ft Hard Severe
A serious and exposed route. Start at the stairway.
1 70ft. 4b. The upper part of the cave can be gained by going through the tunnel into the cave. The tunnel is just above the rock stairway. Alternatively the wall to the left of the tunnel can be climbed to reach the cave. From the right hand side of the cave a rising diagonal traverse leads right over the red wall. Follow this until it fades out, then climb straight up to finish using two vague cracks.

Pot and Glass 90ft Very Severe
Start as for Moss Wall.
1 50ft. Climb the stairway of rock to the good ledge at 10ft. Go right for 5ft until directly below two small caves, one above the other. Climb straight up to the second cave and traverse 5ft right to a slim groove. Follow this to the tree and belay.
2 40ft. From the tree climb diagonally left for 10ft then go straight up to the top and tree belays.

30ft right of the stairway is a large recess in the rock at the foot of the cliff.

Red Shift 100ft Very Severe
A good climb.
1 25ft. Climb the short wall to a groove and continue up this to a large tree and ledge. Belay.
2 75ft. 4c. 5ft left of the tree climb up to a small cave then go up the red wall on the right for a few feet until a traverse line

can be gained, leading to a tiny sapling, 15ft right. From here climb directly up a thin crack for 10ft until a step right to a good ledge and a large sapling can be made. Above this is a fine open groove. Follow this to just below the top where a step onto the right wall is made to finish.

25ft right of the large recess the cliff has a small undercut base. Immediately left of this is a vague crack leading to a groove.

Pam's Pride 100ft Very Severe ★
1 35ft. 4b. Climb the crack and groove to reach a good ledge at 35ft where a stance can be taken.
2 65ft. 4b. From the stance continue up the groove for 20ft until easier rock is reached. Traverse 5ft left into the shallow cave and climb up and out of this to gain the crack and wall above. Climb directly over the finishing overhang. A good climb.

30ft further along the path is a tree at the foot of the crag and just right of this is a groove split by a crack leading to an overhang at 40ft.

Sagitta 100ft Severe
1 100ft. 4a. Climb the groove to the overhang which is best climbed facing left. Above this climb loose rock for 20ft then take the arête on large holds in a fine position to the top.

5ft right of Sagitta is a mossy slab.

An Error of Judgment 60ft Hard Severe
1 60ft. 4a. Go up the mossy slab to an old gnarled root at the foot of a prominent crack. Climb this for 10ft then move right across an arête into another groove and follow this to the top passing some very dubious rock—not a good route.

At the right hand side of this buttress is a fine looking crack which gives the final climb on the crag.

Joyce's Route 50ft Severe
1 50ft. 4a. Climb the crack throughout, exiting right at the top by a sapling in order to avoid an awkward tree.

Index

	page
Albany S	114
An Error of Judgement HS	119
Ankh, The HVS	101
Arch Wall VS	112
Arrow Root D	107
Awopbopalubop Awambamboom VS	115
Bannister VD	111
Beak, The HVS	100
Bell, The HVS	105
Biblin Wall VS	98
Big Bad C HS	104
Big Girl HVS	109
Blackie Boy S	115
Black Tulip XS	102
Bludgeon VS	113
Bookworm S	113
Brittania HS	105
Broken Root MD	108
Bulger, The HS	95
Cave Route HVS	114
Cave Wall VD	94
Central Route VD	117
Chicken Run MD	94
Claptrap VS	113
Cornergrot D	118
Dave's Downfall HS	109
Diamond Groove VS	99
Drunk VS	109
Druid, The VS	103
Exchange MVS	103
Fat Man HS	97
Flying Machine VD	103
Funky Dung VS	94
Funky Gibbon HS	94
Garlic D	94
Geriatrix VS	106
Gerontian VD	113
Gibbon VD	94
Gnome's Groan VS	96

Goblin's Grumble VS	96
Golden Fleece S	103
Green Grow the Grollies Oh! VS	104
Grobbler MVS	103
High Jack HVS	99
Hole in the Wall VS	102
Jewess, The XS	108
Joyce's Route S	119
Jugged Hare D	110
Julep HVD	118
Kebbo S	114
Kipper Crack HS	114
Last Fling HVD	110
Lord of the Dance VS	101
Loony on the Loose MVS	109
Lurcher MVS	110
Mango Highway VS	113
Matchstick Man VS	97
Mellow Yellow HVS	117
Mockingbird VS	100
Moss Wall HS	118
Navvy, The HSV	99
Nikabrik D	110
No Hai VD	113
Odd Bod VD	96
Offspring VS	101
Original Route, The VD	111
Otak HS	108
Overhanging Vee VD	95
Pam's Pride VS	119
Parachute S	107
Peacock MVS	102
Phizzog VS	99
Pierre HVD	95
Porridge VD	110
Pot and Glass VS	118
Priory VS	105
Prow, The VS	111

Index

Red Rose Speedway HVS	101
Red Shift VS	118
Rite Root D	108
Rootin Toot VD	108
Root Route VD	98
Russian, The VS	100
Sagitta S	119
Salutation HS	114
Scooby Doo HVS	100
Sentinel HVD	96
Slidewater Shuffle S	107
Snatch HS	95
Snitch VS	95
Snoozin Suzie VD	98
Staircase VD	111
Strathdon HVS	105
Stress Arete HVS	117
Tea on a Rainy Day HD	112
Travellers Rest D	117
Trip, The HVS	115
Trundlebum Rex VD	104
Twitch HS	95
Vesuvius VS	95
Victory V HVD	94
Wasteland, The XS	101
White Hart HVS	107
Yates VS	105
Yellow Peril HS	117
Yew Stump Corner VD	94
Yew Tree Variations D	95
Yorker HVS	102

New Climbs

WINTOUR'S LEAP

FAR SOUTH BAY

Senta 170ft Very Severe
An obvious groove line between Greta and Zelda, strangely hitherto neglected. Worthwhile, but of less quality than its neighbours.
Start: as for Greta, in the large pit below and left of the prominent corner of Zelda.
1 40ft. 4a. Climb the slab, as for Greta, bearing left to a narrow ledge. Then go straight up to a small stance extending rightwards under an overhang. Poor peg belays.
2 80ft. 4b. Move up and out right of the overhang, up a little, and then back left to the foot of the long groove. Climb the groove and exit left at the top. Traverse 15 feet left and go up on sloping holds to the peg belay shared with Zelda and Greta.
3 50ft. 4b/c. Step up and traverse horizontally right with Zelda as far as an old peg by a borehole on the left of the large nose. Go straight up from here to a ledge and rejoin Zelda for the final 20 foot groove/corner.
Scramble up left to the top of the cliff.
First ascent: John Willson, Paul Curtis Hayward, 1st July 1977

NORTH WALL Some climbers still stray too far left on the last pitch of Left Hand Route. This has now been clearly marked with blue paint.

DECEIVER BUTTRESS A huge chunk of Torment (see appendix) has fallen out of the cliff, giving the lie to my comment about the rock here appearing sounder and underlining the extreme seriousness of this buttress.

FAR SOUTH BAY A hold on the crux of pitch 1 of Zelda has come away revealing a much better one underneath. This is now 4b minus rather than plus and the overall grade should revert to Hard Severe; the 3 star rating stands.

FLY WALL The upper pegs on pitch 1 of The Split have been removed, taking some rock and leaving a useful hold. The pitch is now rather easier at 4c but less well protected. The overall Very Severe grade and the 1 star rating stand.

New Climbs

New Climbs

New Climbs

New Climbs

New Climbs